RED COAT RUNNING
A SHAWN RIGGS NOVEL

BY
CLAYTON J. CALLAHAN

Dedicated to my mother, Delila, who hates science fiction.

Copyright ©. No part of this book may be reproduced by any means without the expressed written consent of the author. This is a work of fiction. Any similarities between the characters hear in or persons living or dead is strictly coincidental.

Cover art by Peter Sega.

Lettering by Patrick Smith of Ignition Design PDX. For more information on Ignition Design PDX, please visit www.ignitiondesignpdx.com.

ISBN: 1548517178

PROLOGUE

My war began after everybody else's had ended.

The wind blew cold while icy rain pelted the windshield of the old army Jeep. The roads were slick but not as bad as they'd been the week before. Pot holes posed a greater danger than ice patches anyway. I swiveled around one big enough to swallow my front tire whole. Shell holes, of course, posed a bigger problem. I didn't dare go above twenty miles an hour for fear of being swallowed up by one of those monsters.

My passenger pointed to the bombed out church on the right. "Pull over here, Shawn. The house is just a few blocks away."

The car slid to a stop as I eased my feet onto the brake and clutch. I could hear the rain patter on the Jeep's canvas roof as I killed the engine and turned off the headlights. Outside, the merciless February wind blew slantwise rain through the unlit Berlin streets. Nobody was taking the air on a night like this. Snuffing out my cigarette, I buttoned up my overcoat and flipped up the collar, bracing for what lay ahead. "Fred, are you sure this is the right neighborhood? Looks like all the houses 'round here have either been pounded to rubble or abandoned."

Fred shrugged. "That's what my contact says. Dr. Gerlatch, Nazi war criminal, living in a two-story brownstone just three blocks over."

"Okay, let's check it out." I pulled my fedora down tight over my head, hoping the wind wouldn't knock it off the moment I stepped outside. "If he's there, we'll get the MPs and do a raid. But if he ain't, you get to tell Lieutenant Dean we lost another one."

"Yes, Corporal Riggs. Roger dodger."

I cast a sideways look at my fellow non-com as I grabbed the door handle. "Smart-aleck."

Stepping out into the cold, my left wing tipped shoe immediately found a deep puddle that soaked my sock in ice water. "Nuts."

Together, Fred and I slogged through the starless night on what remained of the sidewalk. Most of Berlin looked like hell, and only the downtown area had seen much in the way of repairs since the war ended.

We would've avoided streetlights if there were any, but this end of town didn't even have electricity yet. To me, the whole neighborhood resembled a junkyard in a ghost town, and it made my Irish ghetto back in Boston look like Beacon Hill.

We turned a corner, and there it stood, a two-story brownstone at the end of the block. Surrounded by a low stone wall, it had a huge brick fountain in the center of the yard, water frozen in its final ascent. Through the shades, I saw a few flickering candle lights in the front rooms, but the walkway to the front door remained unshoveled, and no cars lined the street. I regarded it as my iced foot lost all feeling in the cold. "Quaint. So what's the plan now, Fred?"

"Plan?"

"My, are you a credit to the Counterintelligence Corps. Yeah, dummy, the plan. Do you want us just to go up and ring the bell? Maybe tell the kraut we're selling subscriptions to Life magazine?"

"At ease, soldier," Fred protested. "Give me a moment to think."

The wind continued to howl in my ears as the rain soaked through the fedora. I'd have loved a cigarette just then, but figured giving away our position might just be a bad idea. Enough operations had gone south these past few months. We didn't need another blot on our record. Besides, it'd be nice if we actually caught one of these Nazi bastards for once. The State Department was especially keen on getting scientists like Gerlach, who'd used Jews in experiments and God knows what else. I'd seen a concentration camp once, and that was enough to motivate anybody with a soul.

"Well," Fred said. "We can just sneak up and look in a window. See if anybody's there and if they are, we go for the MPs."

I couldn't feel my face anymore, so just then, any plan sounded good. I nodded to him, and we advanced on the lonely house at a creep. We got to the front yard, tumbled over the waist-high stone wall, and crept quietly across the snowy lawn past the big frozen fountain.

That's when everything went to hell.

There was a shout in German from inside the house, "Alarm!"

Fred and I dove for cover behind the fountain as a window shattered, and pistol shots rang out in the night air. Frantically, I unbuttoned my coat to reach my gun. An eternity passed as I fumbled through layers of clothing to unholster it. Just as I locked and loaded a round, I heard a car start behind the house. To the left, headlights flicked on. Rolling in the slushy mud, I tried to get a better view, but through the rain, all I could see were three shadows jumping into an old Mercedes. One of those shadows carried a Tommy gun.

The flash of the submachine gun stole my night vision and sent me back to the ground. Bullets roared around me, chipping ice and brick from my best friend in the world at the moment—the fountain. I burrowed deeper into the muck while crossing myself in the name of the Father and the Son. The next sound I heard was the squeal of tires as the car sped off down the street, almost certainly taking a wanted Nazi scientist with it.

Fred's pistol barked eight times into the cold night air, but the car had already spun around a corner. I stood up and shouted, "What the hell are you shooting at?"

"Those guys who shot at us!" Fred answered.

"Well, they're gone now, so knock it off!"

Fred holstered his .45. "You okay, Shawn?"

I just shook my head. "I'm pissed, that's all."

"Yeah," Fred agreed, "people trying to kill you has that effect."

We wiped the mud off our coats…well, some of it anyway. Cold, wet, dirty, and empty-handed, we headed back to the Jeep. Strolling through the slush, my mind went to all the angry places. Somebody had just tried to kill me, and I took that kind of thing personally. "Goddamn, I'd love to go after those guys, but we don't have any other leads, do we?"

Fred shook his head. "No. The only thing I had was a tip about the house."

I smacked my cold fist into a mailbox in frustration and got a good sting for my efforts. "Nuts!"

Fred shrugged. "At least that tip turned out to be a good one this time."

"Somebody warned those bastards, you know?"

"Yep," he agreed. "I think that's a given."

We got in the car, and I slammed the door, rage still burning inside me as I gripped the wheel. "Another loss for Counterintelligence Team Four."

CHAPTER ONE

"Riggs, do you have anything on that Dr. Gerlatch character yet?"

"No, Sir." I supposed Fred hadn't exactly gotten around to telling the boss about last night yet. Lieutenant Dean used to be a patient guy, but the brass at G2 was leaning on him pretty hard.

"You know, Riggs," he said. "It'd be nice to have some good news for a change. Gerlach was supposed to be an easy fish to catch."

"Yes, Sir," I answered.

His eyes went to a telegram in his hand. The news must not have been good. "So, what the hell happened, soldier?"

"I'm sorry, Sir, but all our contacts around him just sort of dried up. We didn't catch him at that house last night." I figured I'd let Fred give him the details on that screw-up later. Dean just stared at me, so I added, "His landlady says she hasn't seen him all week."

"Figures." Dean crumpled up the telegram and tossed it in the burn box as he stormed into his office. If he'd slammed that door it might have fallen off its hinges, so the best he could do was give it a muted thump when he closed it.

The old buildings on Saargemuender Street used to be a German Luftwaffe Headquarters complex. Army engineers had boarded up the broken windows that past spring, but even in the main hall, we could still feel a draft. However, since the lights worked, General Clay had decided to make these red brick monstrosities his Berlin HQ.

The place reminded me of a run down version of Harvard Yard, complete with ivy crawling up the walls but without the fresh-faced college kids. Our rooms lacked anything in the way of plumbing but the front door had a good, secure lock, so I guess that's why we got 'em. Nothing too good for our boys in uniform.

Of course, we didn't always wear our uniforms.

The old radiator finally started to make a difference in the chilly little office as I sat at my plywood desk drinking coffee and reading *Stars and Stripes*. There was nothing more I could do about the Gerlach thing. Besides, it was early in the day, and I hadn't even burned my first cigarette yet. Good thing I had other pots on the burners. I only looked lazy because there was nothing to be done at that particular moment.

On the front page of the paper, I read how British Prime Minister Atlee had just granted India its independence, but I was more interested in the sport's section. The Red Sox were looking good going into spring training. Now that they had Ted Williams back, I was hopeful.

Fred Sands came over to bum a cigarette. Of course, I had one. Maxwell, in supply, still thought he owed me a favor for getting him off that peeper magazine rap. After giving me a full confession, complete with tears and a plea for mercy, I didn't have the heart to tell him that smut was outside of my jurisdiction. Ever since he'd given me first choice of smokes before they ended up at the Post Exchange.

I pulled a fresh pack out of my drawer and busted the seal. "Fred, they sell these things at the PX, you know?"

He smiled as he put the Lucky Strike in his mouth. "Yours are cheaper, Shawn. Hey, aren't you supposed to be meeting with that limey today?"

I looked at my watch. "He's not due for another half an hour. I've got time to kill."

"Good, can I borrow your typewriter? Mine's got an 'h' that sticks."

"Fred, why the hell don't you just borrow my socks and skivvies while you're at it?" I shook my head. Fred was needy, but he wasn't a bad guy. He spoke three languages, so he wasn't entirely useless either. Me, I just spoke some French badly, and English fluently. Even then, folks outside of Boston sometimes didn't understand me. Oh, and I had a few phrases of Gallic in my head, but what the hell good was that? As to German, I'd learned "hello," "goodbye," and that was about it after three months in the country.

I picked up the old Underwood typewriter and handed it to Fred. "It probably needs a new ribbon. Swap it out, and I'll take the box down to the burn barrel. It's getting full anyway."

Stretching as I got up, I went to the old ammo box where we chucked all the spent typewriter tape and draft documents. Fred dropped the last one in, and I took the box outside to the barrel. It was a crisp March morning, clear and beautiful without a cloud in the sky. Germany's weather wasn't that much different from that in Massachusetts, so I didn't mind it. Fred Sands, however, was from Arizona. He hated it.

A garden wall closed off the back of the building, so nobody was going to bother me. I dumped the contents of the box into the fifty-five-gallon drum and put my Zippo to work. While the flames licked at the evidence of our post-war adventures, I kicked back against the wall and lit a cig for myself.

As I breathed in the smoke, I thought, this isn't bad duty at all…working in an office, wearing civilian clothes some days, and nobody had ordered me to do a push-up in months. Sure, we still had to do morning formations in front of the first sergeant, but that was as "army" as most of our days got.

When all the documents and ribbons were destroyed, I snuffed out my cigarette and went back to the office. The MI6 agent was already sitting at my desk, smoking a hand-rolled cigarette, the kind they didn't sell at the PX.

"Top of the morning; you must be Mr. Leer," I said as I extended my hand.

He rose and took it. "I have that privilege, sir."

His gray-brown tweed suit looked as nondescript as tenement wallpaper. Blond hair with just the right amount of cream crowned a long, angular head with a prominent nose.

"I'm Riggs, Shawn Riggs, US Army Special Agent. I spoke with you on the phone."

"Yes, pleasure to make your acquaintance. I read your reports as well, and I do believe you know most of the particulars. I require you to be at the Cafe Komfort at three o'clock sharp, today, in civilian attire."

I glanced down at my brown army class-B uniform and shrugged. "I have a suit that should do fine. I drove past the cafe yesterday with an MP patrol. It's easy to find, just the other side of Stresemann Street. It won't be a problem, Mr. Leer."

"Nigel," he winced. "Just call me Nigel. I take it you didn't draw attention to yourself yesterday?"

I shook my head. "Can't see how. I was just another Joe in a Jeep, and we were able to merge with a passing convoy."

"Lucky you. Still, one can never be too careful. I must insist you be discreet."

"Hey, it ain't like I'm going to wear my badge in plain view," I told him.

Now it was the Brit's turn to shake his head. "Americans and their badges. What is it with you people, hmm?"

I shrugged. "It comes in handy sometimes."

"A handy way to get yourself burned, old man. Your OSS chaps didn't feel the need for those silly little things."

"I wouldn't know about that." I'd never worked with the Office of Strategic Services. "Counterintelligence Corps has 'em is all."

"Very well," he said as he snuffed out his fine cigarette on my cheap desk. I didn't mind. The government desk already had a lot of scratches, marks, and stains anyway. My desk had been in the war; I hadn't.

Taking a moment to look me in the eye, he said, "Just be discreet, old man. Nobody knows me in that part of Berlin, and I want to keep it that way."

I nodded. Nigel picked up his black porkpie cap from my desk, put it on top of his perfect blond hair, and went his way. I always pictured Englishmen as mean little buggers with bad teeth. And to hear Grandpa Dullahan talk, they were. But Grandpop may have been a bit prejudiced by his time in the Irish Republican Brotherhood.

I knocked on Lieutenant Dean's door and told him about the operation. He very much wanted one thing to go right before he rotated home. With so many other things botched, he needed to get this last bit of business over with. I didn't blame him. We hadn't exactly been the shining stars of the spy world, and the State Department was calling for our butts.

A lot of our job had been making contact with German scientists or political types that the State Department boys wanted to chew the fat with. Problem was, these guys kept disappearing. Rumor had it that they were slipping away to Argentina, or that the Jews were hunting them down and killing 'em. Not that I would blame Jews for that, but I didn't exactly believe either set of stories. None of the guys we were looking for had the dough to make it to South America, and the Jews I saw in Germany were either dying in the hospitals or dying to get to Palestine.

Somebody was eating our lunch.

***

That afternoon I sat in a battered chair at a rinky-dink table, wearing my second best blue pinstriped suit and a tan trench coat. Welcome to the Cafe Komfort; Russian Sector, not that it mattered back then. The Ruskies were still, sort of, kind of, our allies back in '46.

I watched some errant leaves blow past the rubble and wondered where they'd come from. Then I remembered Tiergarten Park, the one with all the statues just a block away. The statues were toppled in the fighting—or in the Russians' celebrations after the fighting; I couldn't say which. Great Kaisers of the past etched in garnet and bronze, all face down in the mud as Fräuleins planted potatoes around them. It had been a hard winter; people had starved.

The waiter walked over in a pressed white uniform jacket. It impressed me that he managed to keep it so clean, and it would be a few more years before another dry cleaner opened in Berlin. I tried to order a cup of tea, knowing there was no way they'd have coffee. Unfortunately, his English was worse than my German, so I pointed to the customer at the next table who was having a cup and made drinking motions with my hands. He got the message. I looked at my watch; 1543 hours, or 3:43 p.m. to the civilians of the world. Where the hell was Nigel?

The waiter returned with the tea faster than I expected. I said one of the few German words I knew. "Danke."

"You're welcome, Mr. Riggs, but I thought I told you to be discreet."

I did a double take. There was Nigel where the waiter should have been. He wasn't wearing his suit jacket or hat, but had rolled up his shirtsleeves, lost his tie, and draped a towel over his arm. Not exactly the spit and polish of the real waiter's outfit, but he could pass for a cafe employee, no problem. "Holy cow. Where've you been?"

"In the back of the cafe where casual eyes wouldn't see me. Not out on the street, old man, like a working girl looking for a tryst." He gently shook his head and handed me the bill. "Pay me."

"What?" I asked.

"Pay the bill, Mr. Riggs. I'm your waiter."

I blinked a few times, but I did manage to reach into my pocket and pull out a pack of cigarettes. I left six on the table. That would cover the bill and add a healthy tip. Nobody was using Deutsche Marks in Germany just yet.

Nigel took the cigarettes but left the bill. He walked brusquely back toward the kitchen, like a busboy who had a lot of work to do. I glanced at the bill. There were instructions.

I have found out she is leaving town today. I've been told she may be selling her furniture for traveling money. The Burkhoft Furniture Store is closest to her apartment and is two blocks north and one block east. Be there, but for God's sake, be discreet!

Discreet is not an easy thing to be when you're the only guy in Germantown with a full belly and all your arms and legs still attached. I grew up poor, but not like these Krauts; they weren't poor, they were broken. The few men of military age walking the streets often did so with one leg and two crutches. I stood out.

Looking around, I spotted a lucky winner from across the street. He was probably a young kid, but he looked about sixty. He wore a battered, oversized Nazi coat with all the goo-gahs removed, and a stocking cap his grandmother might have knitted for him. Crossing the street, I smiled as I approached him.

"Hey, Mac, you speak English?"

He stopped in his tracks and looked down at his toes. "Yes."

I was in luck. "Good, I want to buy your coat and hat. How much?"

"Yes." He still didn't look up.

I blinked. "Yes, what?"

"Yes."

"Great."

I took off my trench coat...I had to make this quick. I thrust the coat in his face. He looked up uncomprehendingly. I grabbed his coat's lapel and gave it a tug. The kid nodded, and we traded. Next, I took off my fedora. It was a nice hat, and I was going to miss it, but Lieutenant Dean was right. We were long overdue for a successful operation.

The kid seemed reluctant at first. Maybe his grandmother really did knit the hat for him? But when I flashed the rest of my pack of cigarettes, the last of his resistance broke. He gave me his hat, took the fedora and the cigs from me, and then ran down the street as fast as he could before the crazy American could change his mind. I wished him well with a scrap of my puny German vocabulary. "Auf wiedersehen, buddy."

The coat stank of sweat and I didn't know what else. Too bad for me. I put it on and donned the knit cap. I read Nigel's directions one more time and headed north, taking care to rip up the bill he'd given me. I scattered some of the pieces on the ground, others I shoved in my pocket, and a few I ate. Changing my gait, I scrambled along like a defeated German, not some strutting GI.

The furniture store was the only intact shop in a busted up old building. I figured the owner probably knew the place was due for demolition, so he didn't even bother putting up curtains. Through the store windows, I could see a fine selection of merchandise; regal looking couches and chairs that probably came from what were once the finest homes in Berlin. I wondered what my mom would do in a place like that; she always could spot a bargain.

Walking into the store would probably be too obvious. Besides, I had no idea how long I'd have to wait. So, I found a nice piece of sidewalk and curled up to take a nap like any respectable Teutonic bum might do.

Now, I hated waiting, especially when I didn't even have a paper to read. Still, it was part of the job, and dad had always told me to do a good job. Before the war, my father worked as a teamster out of the stables by Quincy Market. I remember him smiling as he drove that wagon around town, proud as a peacock. He delivered milk mostly, until he'd lost that job. That was when everybody lost their jobs. Dad did what he could. He dug ditches, did odd jobs for the neighbors, and worked on the docks for a bit, but nothing really lasted. He figured if he did a good enough job somewhere they'd keep him, but the trouble wasn't him. There just wasn't much work for a mick back then. Everywhere there were signs in shop windows, INNA—Irish Need Not Apply. Finally, he went to work for Bugs Dwyer...but he didn't like that kind of work.

    The old Nazi coat chafed my neck, but I kept the collar up anyway; it hid my face. I watched the shop until it started to get dark, checking my watch as the time crawled by. At 1830 hours she finally showed up, pushing a cart full of old furniture. She had a few chairs, an end table, and maybe a footstool. It was all nice stuff, well upholstered. Too bad for her. She might have gotten a pretty penny for it.

    She wore a good brown coat and a snappy black beret, like the French wear, but her face wasn't snappy. Her face was drawn and tired like the rest of the Germans; only she wasn't a German. She was some dumb-assed broad from New Jersey who'd joined the Bund back in the thirties before Hitler was officially our enemy. I didn't know what her hang up was. Maybe she was just one of those lug-heads who hated the Jews for some damn reason. I didn't know, and I didn't care. Whatever her reasons, she'd sure made a spectacle of herself on the radio these past five years. Her name was Mildred Gillars, but as I crossed the street, I addressed her by her other name.

    "Hello, Axis Sally."

    She stopped cold in her tracks and terror raced into her eyes, but I wasn't there to comfort her. I reached in my back pocket and pulled out the badge. "US Army, Special Agent Riggs, ma'am. You're under arrest."

As Mildred let go of her cart, I pocketed my badge. When I looked up, I couldn't help but notice the pistol pointed at my gut. Her hands shook, but the barrel of the Walther P-38 stayed in a direct line to my stomach. A flush of anger coursed through my veins, but the only thing I had to say was, "Shit."

The safety flicked off, and my head snapped up to look her in the face. Her eyes narrowed.

This was it.

Suddenly a masculine hand reached over her shoulder to cover the gun, and the barrel turned up. "I'll be taking that, mum." With a twist, Nigel disarmed the dame and handed me the pistol.

"Thanks," I said, putting the gun in my belt as relief washed over me. "I didn't see you here."

"Kind of the point, hmm. I didn't see you at first either. That is until I noticed a vagrant checking his watch."

Nuts, I thought; bums don't have watches. That was stupid of me. "Just trying to be discreet," I answered. Our attention went back to the traitor.

We both had her boxed in pretty good. She didn't try to run and didn't try to plead or say anything at all. The terror slunk out of her eyes as it realized there was just no point in sticking around. Maybe she just gave up, her last hope gone. Looking at me with the vacant, hollow eyes of someone who hadn't eaten or slept regularly in a long time, she silently begged for mercy. I knew that look. I'd seen it on a few concentration camp survivors. I didn't have any pity for the bitch, but I didn't feel good about busting her either. I was just a working stiff doing my job.

Taking hold of her arm, I walked her the six blocks to where my car was parked. Well, not my car exactly, but I did sign for it when Uncle Sam issued it to me. It was one of them

Mercedes, dented up a bit, with tires that didn't match, but it ran okay. I think it used to belong to some German officer. I think the German officer was dead.

Nigel kept pace.

"I owe you one, Nigel."

"Piffle, just doing my duty for king and country."

"So, where were you all this time?" I asked.

He smiled. "A magician doesn't reveal his tricks, old man. Still, I gather you can guess since you seem to know something of the art as well."

I flipped the scratchy coat collar from my neck. "I just figured a change of clothes would make me more discreet."

"Nothing like a bit of polish to aid in that."

"What?" I asked.

"Polish, old man, your disguise. We say you've polished, in MI6."

"Oh, I didn't know that," I replied. "It just seemed like a good idea at the time."

"Good, follow the old instincts. We'll make a proper spy out of you yet." He snuffed out his cigarette on my hood and stepped away from the car.

I smiled and waved goodbye while I opened the door for Berlin's former top radio host. Nigel gave me a tip of his hat, turned, and walk away. I had no idea where his car was parked, but I doubted if he would let me find out. Security, you know, old man, pish-posh and what-what.

Too tired to run and too exhausted to care, the traitor got in the car without a word. Fine by me, I didn't feel particularly chatty. I lit a cigarette but didn't offer her one as I drove to the military police station. What I really could use was a sandwich. I hadn't eaten since breakfast.

The MPs were set up in an old Gestapo office in the American Sector—of course. I parked the battered Mercedes next to a row of shiny new Jeeps and escorted Miss Gillars into the stone building through the front door. Behind the desk sat a sergeant first class, about ten years older than me, and twenty pounds fatter. His MP armband sagged from his left sleeve.

"Special Agent Riggs, US Army. I got a prisoner for ya."

"Special Agent who?" the sergeant replied in a thick southern accent.

"Riggs," I answered as I threw up my badge.

The sergeant squinted. "What's that badge say?"

I glanced at it, although I knew what it said. "War Department, Military Intelligence."

He shook his head. "It don't say special agent."

"No."

"Then why you say you a special agent, if the badge don't say you a special agent?"

I snorted. "It says military intelligence because that's what I am. I'm a counterintelligence agent in the US Army, and I'm bringing you a prisoner. This woman is an American traitor, and she's under arrest."

"You in the army?"

I rolled my eyes. "Yes, I'm in the goddamn army."

"Now watch your mouth with me, boy, I'm a platoon sergeant!" Then, thinking better of it, he asked, "What rank are you?"

Actually, I was a T-corporal, which meant that this jerk outranked me by quite a few steps, but I wasn't about to let him confuse his rank with my authority. "My rank is special agent. Now this is an MP station, right?"

He nodded.

"Good, then I have a prisoner for you to take into custody. Lock her up, and I'll get started on the paperwork."

"You gonna' do the paperwork?" he asked.

Jesus, Mary, and Joseph, how did this jerk make first class? "Yes, that's what I said."

"Well, okay then. Ya don't need to get testy." The sergeant called up a few privates, and they took Axis Sally to a cell while I found a typewriter.

Ironic, I was just a draftee that got snagged in the last years of the war. But I ended up with this weird intelligence gig for one critical reason...I could type. When I was going through basic training at Fort Devens, this guy I never saw before came into our barracks with my drill sergeant. I still remember wondering if I should go to attention or parade rest when he walked in. For sergeants, you had to stand at parade rest, but this guy didn't have any stripes on his sleeves. For officers, you had to stand at attention, but he didn't have any rank on his collar either...just the letters US.

The guy asked who could type and I raised my hand. I'd learned in high school. They gave me a typing test, and I must've done pretty well because I finished five minutes ahead of everybody else. I got transferred to the Counterintelligence Corps after I finished boot camp. It turned out there was a lot of typing involved in being a spy.

Who knew?

A lot of typing indeed, I wasn't finished with all the reports on Axis Sally until 0115 hours the next day. At least the MPs gave me some coffee and donuts. I didn't even mind that the coffee was lousy and the donuts stale. Counterintelligence Team Four had finally won a victory.

CHAPTER TWO

Nigel and I had coffee at my office a few times after that, but we didn't do any more missions together. When the British and American Zones combined in late '46, my team was transferred. It took us three weeks to get all our gear packed up and shoved in the back of duce-and-a-half trucks headed to France. I didn't ever expect to see our old digs at Berlin HQ again. But that's the army; you go where they tell you and you don't ask why.

But I was glad of it. Our new office was in Paris—sort of. The Island of St. Germane was an oversized, mosquito-infested sand spit in the river Seine that the liberated French were only too glad to give the US Army as a campsite. The clapboard barracks and tin-roofed chow hall were hardly the Ritz Carlton, but at least there was a PX and a movie theater.

Team Four's building was just another barracks house like the rest, except ours sported blacked out windows. On the plus side, unlike the Berlin post, each agent had a separate office to work out of. I was even able to score a nice coffee table and couch for mine, certain that General Clay would never miss 'em.

Lieutenant Dean left us in late 1947, his tour up and his ticket punched. He was a good guy, but the new boss wasn't a tool either. Chief Warrant Officer Reynardie was ex-OSS, and he knew his stuff inside and out. He'd spent the war working with the Italian resistance doing things he couldn't tell even us about. He seemed to need a break, and the army had given him a nice soft post. Our workload stayed kind of light for our first six months there.

Most days we just sat around reading old reports and drinking coffee.

Unfortunately, by 1948 things weren't going so well for Europe on the whole. Now that the war was over, the Russians didn't seem to want to be our friends anymore. Maybe they never really wanted to be our friends in the first place, who knows? Suddenly, we were investigating every US soldier who may have ever been a Communist; especially the ones with placement and access to classified material. I knew a few Reds back in Boston; labor agitators and college kids who passed out handbills at breadlines and such. I thought they were pretty harmless back then. But to the army, now they were all suspected traitors. So as the summer of '48 rolled around, we were up to our armpits in interviews and investigations. Too bad for me.

My phone rang. "Agent Riggs, your 1300 appointment is here," said the private at the front desk.

"Okay, send him in."

I buttoned the top button on my khaki shirt with the US on the collars and straightened my tie, then grabbed a notebook and put it on the coffee table. In a minute flat, I heard a knock on my door.

"Come in."

A scared looking guy in a uniform like mine opened the door, but he didn't come in. He just stood there wringing his garrison hat in his hands. On his left collar was a gold bar, and on his right the castle emblem of the Army Engineer Corps. "Second Lieutenant Bob Manley, reporting as ordered, Sir."

"Good morning, Lieutenant." I gave him a genuine smile and waved him in. "Please, have a seat. Would you like a cup of joe?"

The young officer stepped in and found a seat on one of the couches. "Uh—"

"Coffee, Lieutenant, French stuff. I got at the Notre Dame market last Sunday. It's pretty good."

"Thanks, Sir," he stammered. "I'll take it with cream if you got it."

I nodded. "Of course I've got it—nothing but the best for our boys in uniform." I poured two cups and handed him the one with the cream. Then, I plopped on the other couch and pulled my badge from my pocket. "I'm Special Agent Riggs, US Army Counterintelligence Corps. But you can call me Shawn. I'm going to be asking you about your political affiliations prior to joining the army. All right?"

"Yes, Sir."

I smiled at him. "It's Shawn."

"Yes, Shawn."

"Good, so you like baseball?" I got him to loosen up by chewing the fat for a while. I was in no hurry, and I'd learned scared people don't tell you much anyway. I gave him some ribbing about Bucky Harris when I found out he was a Yankee's fan. He thought Bucky was doing a fine job and was gonna give the Red Sox a run for their money. I had to disagree, but I stayed friendly about it. The lieutenant finished the coffee. I poured him another cup, and we got down to cases.

I asked him about the labor group he was involved in back at New York University. Yes, it was a Communist group. And yes, he knew that at the time. He attended a few meetings, but when his finals came up, he didn't have time for it anymore. I asked him if he still considered himself a Communist, and he said he never really considered himself one in the first place.

"I just went to the meetings because I had some friends that went. We'd drink beer and stuff. I guess they were a bit more serious about it than I was."

This wasn't getting me anywhere so I started to turn up the heat. "So, if I told you I have a witness that says you were once this group's treasurer, you would say the witness is lying?"

His eyes narrowed, and his cheeks wrinkled up quizzically. "Who told you that?"

"Just answer the question, please."

He shook his head. "I was never the treasurer. I don't think the group even had one."

I leaned in from across the coffee table and spread my hands open to him. "Bob, you're a good guy. I want to help you out, man to man. But I can't help you if you lie to me. Now, just be jake. You weren't just there for the beer."

"I was there because my friends were there. I told you that."

I picked up my notebook and pretended to review the things I'd written down. "You say you first went to a meeting in December of 1944?"

He shook his head. "No, I said it was sometime in the spring, maybe April of '45?"

"But you're not sure?"

"No. Like I said, it wasn't that important to me. I went to a lot of different kinds of club meetings my freshman year. I was just trying to get to know people."

That matched my notes. His story was consistent, but I wasn't going to let him on to that. I closed the notebook with a snap and slammed it on the coffee table. "Bob, I'm trying to help you, damn it! There's more to this and you know it. If you come clean now, I can keep you out of the stockade. But it's a once in a lifetime offer, pal. You get it?"

Lieutenant Manley stood up. "I told you everything!"

"And you're willing to stake your future on that?"

He looked me in the eye with a cold stare. "Yes. Now if you don't mind, Special Agent Shawn, I got work to do back at my unit!"

He put his garrison cap on and stormed out of my office. As the plywood door slammed shut, I smiled. He really was a good guy. Naturally, all that stuff I made up about him being the group's treasurer was complete malarkey. All I really had on him was a report from one of his own troops that he'd mentioned he went to a Communist meeting once back in college. But Manley didn't take the bait and he didn't get scared. He got mad. Honest people always get mad at the end when they're accused of lying. Dirty people get mad at the beginning, and then they try to make a deal when they think they're gonna get nailed. The lieutenant didn't try to make a deal; he let the chips fall where they may, confident he was innocent.

I gulped down the last of my cold coffee and checked my watch. 1530 hours; that was a long interview. I undid my cuffs and rolled up my sleeves. Time to get typing: *Subject—2nd LT Robert Manley, Disposition—Returned to duty without prejudice, Date—June 10, 1948.*

***

"Shawn, aren't you done typing yet? We gotta' get."

Fred Sands poked his head into my office as I looked at my watch. I'd been working for three hours on the Lieutenant Manley report and missed chow. The heck with it, reports weren't due until twenty-four hours after the interviews anyway. I could finish in the morning; Paris awaited.

Fred and I walked back to our barracks to change shirts. It was still good to be an American GI in France in those days. The locals still loved us, and the uniform was worth at least one free drink and maybe a kiss when out on the town. Our duty shirts just had the letters US on the lapel, but we didn't wear those when we went out. On the town, people sometimes noticed the lack of rank on our sleeves and started asking questions—and when you had a few beers in, you just might screw up and give 'em answers. So, I put on my other shirt, the one with the buck-sergeant stripes, and headed out the door with Staff Sergeant Fred Sands.

Sands smirked as he looked at my arm. "About time you got them T-Corporal stripes taken off, Shawn."

"Hey, I've been busy."

"Doing what…your nails, pretty-boy?"

"No, smart-ass," I protested. "Brushing up on my high school French. It takes more than good looks to score in Paris."

"Well, you do have that boyish charm thing working for you, and I reckon you ain't too short," Sands quipped.

"Five-seven isn't short!"

"Uh-huh," he prodded further. "At least you ain't all red-haired and freckle-faced like First Sergeant McGuire."

Most of my neighborhood looked like our first sergeant, and I didn't see anything wrong with that. But Fred had never been to Boston. "I'm black Irish," I told him.

Sands's eyebrows knitted together. "You ain't a negro."

"Now you're being a dumb-ass, Fred." Well, what's a guy from Arizona supposed to know? "Black Irish means I got ancestors who were part of the Spanish Armada way back when. They got shipwrecked off the coast of Ireland and never went home. They stayed and married the local girls; that's where I got the black hair."

"So you're an Irishman with Spanish roots, but you don't speak Irish or Spanish?"

I shrugged. "Like I said, a little Gallic, some high school French, and how to say 'hello' and 'good-bye' in German…maybe."

"Well, let's see how well you parlay," he smiled. "I heard about this jazz club said to be full of high-class fems. Called 'Le Boeuf Sur—something,' just about a three-mile walk."

Fred and I strolled across the bridge and entered the city proper. The weather was warm and the breeze fresh. I'd heard people complain about the smell in Paris, but I guess there was something about being from Boston that just killed all the senses in my nose. We stopped at a cafe and got some dinner. Fred laughed when I tried to order, but the waiter understood me well enough.

"Hey, buddy, not everybody's dad worked for the State Department, ya' know?"

Fred chuckled. "Well, I didn't pick up all my languages traveling overseas with Dad. Mexico was just about ten miles from our hometown. You're from the big city. Didn't folks come from all over the world to be your neighbor?"

I shook my head. "In Boston, you keep to your own. The only other language I heard spoken was Italian, and I usually heard it when some bruiser was shouting at me to get my ass back to my own neighborhood. Good thing Reynardie's from New York; no connection to the punks I knew."

Fred leaned in. "Gangsters?"

"Not like in the movies." Now he was getting personal. "Nobody carried Tommy guns or anything like that. I got a knife pulled on me a couple of times, but that's all."

Fred shrugged. "Seems like that would be enough."

"Well, it sure pissed me off at the time." I had an Irish temper. When I got mad, I tended to stay mad for a long time. It was not a good trait.

We finished the meal and strolled the extra five or six blocks to the club. It was a modest looking place from the outside, but it did take up two storefronts and had a big picture window with a crack running down it.

Inside, the joint was huge with a two-story ceiling, bright yellow walls, and lots of room. It was maybe eight or nine o'clock by then, and the place was starting to jump. A band played swing, and about half the dance floor was full. When the maître d' saw our uniforms, he led us to a table right up front and brought us each a beer on the house. The beer went down cold, and the swing was hot. Some French gal with a great set of pipes belted out Dick Haymes's *Little White Lies* in French with a full horn section backing her up.

We sat there for a while just enjoying the scene; then this dame walked in wearing a red dress and a wide smile.

Seeing her blonde hair, full hips, and a chest well-endowed by nature, my mind went right to sin number one on the list of seven deadly. Her moves were custom designed to focus all eyes on her, and mine followed like the rest. Then—a miracle, it seemed—she sat at the table right next to ours. I hardly noticed the man in the tan suit who sat down behind her.

She winked at us. "Americans! And so handsome."

"You speak English?" I stammered.

"But, of course." Her smile was warm and intimate as her shoulders leaned in, pushing her bosom up front and center.

She was every pin-up girl in the barracks just then, and somehow I got up the nerve to ask her to dance. As I took her hand, Sands muttered, "You big dope. You don't even know how to dance."

"Shut-up!" I whispered as Aphrodite, and I took to the floor.

Sands was right; I couldn't dance. So she and I did the three steps I knew over, and over, and over again. She laughed but not in a mean way, her chest jiggling all the while. Damn, it was good to be a GI in Paris!

When the song ended, we went back to the tables. Fred found a pretty little Indo-China girl and was cutting a rug with her, while I ordered more beer for my lady friend and me. We chatted and laughed, her French accent adding to her overall allure. She was very direct and soon got right to the point.

"You have known many women, yes?"

I blushed. "No."

"No?" She giggled.

I'd never been a Casanova in high school. Truth was, women made me a bit nervous, and I never knew how to get things started. Gals expected a fellow to take the lead, and I could never figure out how to do that without sounding like an ass. If this French beauty hadn't come up to me like she did, we probably wouldn't even be talking.

I shook my head. "None."

"Oh my-my, this is going to be fun." She smiled and leaned in closer. Her boobs rose like bubbles in a champagne glass, and my little soldier stood at attention. "We go back to my apartment? We have some fun?"

I smiled and tried not to sound too eager. "Yes."

She batted her eyes. "And my husband, he can watch?"

That night I slept in my bunk back at the barracks. I won't say I went right to sleep, but I did sleep with a clean conscience.

And I looked forward to boring the hell out of some priest the next time I went to confession.

***

The next morning, after formation, I sat in Reynardie's office with Ecklan, the new guy, and Fred Sands. I'd finished my report just after breakfast and put it in the boss's "in" box, but Reynardie probably wouldn't read it 'til after lunch. We were smoking cigs, drinking coffee, and generally just shooting the shit while the boss went through the daily reports; pretty much the start of any normal day.

Of the three of us, only Ecklan was working on anything interesting. One of those ambitious career guys, he worked fast and already had a source inside the French Ministry of Defense who gave him dope on one of their colonies in Asia. Of course, we weren't supposed to collect on our allies, but after the way the Ruskies flipped on us our higher at G2 was willing to look the other way. I had no grudge against his success; I just wished he wasn't so goddamned arrogant about it. Then again, Ecklan was goddamned arrogant about most things. He was one of those guys who acted like he had all the answers and nobody else ever knew squat. What a jackass.

Chief Reynardie looked up from his desk. "So, Shawn, that engineer LT check out okay?"

I put my coffee cup down on the armrest. "Yep, he's just some dumb kid who knocked back a few brews with some Reds in college. No current affiliation, no placement or access to classified material, no risk to national security."

"You sure, son?" Reynardie asked. "Command is getting awfully touchy about these things nowadays."

I shrugged. In this business, it's not possible to be one-hundred percent sure about anybody, so I didn't see any point in pretending. "He didn't trip over his dick. I interviewed him for over two hours. My gut says he's clean. He's either on the level or one well trained Commie spy."

Ecklan chipped in his two cents. "It's called tradecraft, Riggs. They do train spies in that kind of thing, you know?"

I just glared at him.

"Hmm," Reynardie snorted and went back to his reading. He'd pulled me and Ecklan apart a few times before, and he was letting us know he was in no mood for that shit now. That was fine by me.

I picked up my coffee cup and raised it to my lips.

Reynardie asked, "Riggs, you ever meet a limey named Nigel Leer?"

The coffee paused in front of my face, asking itself if it wanted to be drunk or not. I put it back down while it made up its mind. "Yeah, I worked with him on that Axis Sally thing over two years ago. What about him?"

"Brits just sent us a report that he's gone rogue. Seems he's been moonlighting as a Bolshevik since who-knows-when. MI6 was just his day job."

My jaw dropped so low it almost knocked the coffee cup off the armrest. Ecklan and Sands stared at me as if I'd suddenly grown a second nose. This was not a good time of year to admit you knew a Red spy, especially when you just let a pinko lieutenant off the hook. Of all the eloquent things I was capable of saying, my mouth just let out, "Awe, nuts."

Sands filled the gap. "The Brits have been on top of this game for a long time, boss. They even helped us get the old OSS up and running back in your day. How the hell did they let this guy slip past?"

Reynardie nodded. "I got my first real schooling at Bletchley Park with some of their boys; top-notch training too. But I guess even His Royal Majesty has bad days like everybody else."

"How did they catch him?" I wanted to know.

Reynardie sent his eyes back to the paper on his desk. "They didn't, at least not yet. He was found out through a source on the other side four days ago. Scotland Yard's still looking for him in

Great Britain, but MI5 seems to think he slipped out of the country using a false passport just yesterday. He's traveling under the name of David Lane."

"And they think he's trying to make it to Russia?" Ecklan asked.

The boss shrugged. "That would make sense. I don't know where else he'd go."

"What was his placement and access?" I wanted to know.

Reynardie bit his lower lip as his eyes went back to the paper. "Shucks. His last post was chief of the central European station. Son-of-a-bitch would know every Allied agent we got running in that neck of the woods."

Ecklan was on the edge of his seat. "You think he's already given that information to the Russians?"

I thought about it. Nigel had been a very careful guy. Reynardie said he only got burnt because someone on the other side gave him up. If he had information, he wouldn't send it by radio. Having a transmitter in your house was a lot more damning than carrying a badge in your pocket. He couldn't send it by telephone or telegram because it would be too likely to be intercepted. Reynardie had once said the safest way to get information out was to work through dead drops and couriers. But now that Nigel was on the lam, he'd have no way of re-establishing contact without putting his comrades at risk.

No, the odds were he took whatever information he was saving and ran with it. All the stuff that would've been too risky to leak before he'd have to hand-carry it to Mother Russia. That kind of information might mean the difference between a house by the Black Sea or a shack in Siberia to a guy like him. Of course, all of this was guesswork. I had no way to be sure, but it would be what I would've done in his shoes.

Reynardie answered Ecklan's question. "I don't know if he's passed it on yet. But the Brits want him back real bad. This report reads like an Old West wanted poster; dead or alive."

I looked up. "If he left England he probably went straight to France or Belgium. Ferries cross the Channel all the time, and nobody would think much of an Englishman going on holiday. From there the fastest way east would be by train. All the French rail lines eventually go through Paris. It ain't Nigel's only option, but it's a good one."

"Nigel? You on a first name basis with this Commie?" Ecklan asked.

What an asshole. Why did this guy try to make everything a confrontation? All I could do was shrug.

The boss seemed to mull that over. He took a sip of his coffee. I'd abandoned mine to its fate. "Shawn, you think you can recognize this palooka?"

"Yes, Sir."

"Good." He put the report down. "Get into civies and run your ass down to Gare Du Nord. That's the biggest train station in town, so the odds favor it." Reynardie pinched the bridge of his nose like he had a headache coming on. "That's if he's even coming through Paris at all. You see him, call back and let us know what train he got on. We can pass the information down the line, and the French Gendarmes can arrest him at the next stop. Too easy."

I shrugged and stood up. "Too easy, boss."

I went back to my barracks room and changed out of uniform and into my best gray double-breasted suit. My mother had sent it to me in a care package for my birthday last December, and it looked damn good on me. I wore my pale tie, covered in little black diamonds, and a simple gray fedora to complete the outfit.

I looked around for anything else I might need. Mail call must have happened while I was out because someone had left a letter from my father on my bunk. "Swell," I said as I tucked it into my jacket pocket next to my shoulder holster. Under my left arm, I wore the standard Army Colt .45. I never had a call to use the thing, but Dad carried a rod back when he worked for Bugs, so I figured it was a good idea. I shoved my badge into my pants pocket. It came in handy, and besides, it would be an Article Fifteen offense if I lost it. I also grabbed my passport so I wouldn't have to show military ID to anybody unless I wanted to. As I walked out of the barracks, I almost forgot that I'd left my wallet in my uniform pants. I turned back to grab it. I'd gotten some back pay for my promotion last week, and I hadn't even had the chance to get to the finance office to bank it or to change it into francs. Fortunately, I had a few unspent francs from my night out, so I was set.

I checked my watch; 0830 hours. No telling how soon Nigel would make it to the station—if he was going to the station—if he was in France at all.

My Mercedes had been re-issued to some big-shot major when we left Berlin. We had no wheels for the Paris office. I could have a private drive me to the station in a Jeep, but no, that would be stupid. So I took a walk across the bridge and waited for the crosstown bus. In just under forty-five minutes, my ass was at the Gare Du Nord train station just like the chief ordered.

***

It was busy, as train stations always were; a couple hundred people getting on and off under the arched steel girders, most dressed in suits topped with fedoras or those funny black berets; a few tradesmen wore leather jackets. The station staff were all dressed in blue uniforms with old-fashioned pillbox hats. A young panhandler gave me the squeeze. He understood enough English to call me an "asshole" when I didn't give him any dough.

The best place to watch the station was from the main platform, right on the spot where a plaque announced a German general had surrendered to de Gaulle three years back. Trouble with that location was I could be seen as well as see from there, and Nigel was no amateur. So I decided to do a roving patrol of the platform instead.

I strolled around at a leisurely pace, occasionally stopping to buy a croissant from a cart or a newspaper from the newsstand. It was actually a pretty boring way to spend the morning, and I started to wonder how long Reynardie expected me to play this gig. Taking a break against a lamppost, I opened the paper. It was in French so I couldn't read much of it, but it provided cover, and I blended in with the crowd okay. There was a picture of President Truman on the front page. I doubted the frogs were saying anything nice about him. Everybody missed FDR.

I happened to glance up, and a funny looking beret caught my eye. I didn't know why I focused on it at first, but it just sort of stood out. Then I realized I wasn't looking at a beret; it was a black porkpie cap. What were the odds? Well, that day they were pretty damn good because, in that instant, I caught a glimpse of Nigel walking away from the ticket counter.

I had to be careful; Nigel knew my face. I stood stark still, watching him over the edge of my newspaper. He wore a tweed jacket with a gray turtleneck sweater underneath. It was a cool summer day, but that was dressing a might warm for the weather. He carried no luggage, and his hands were in his pockets like he didn't have a care in the world. I watched him carefully, but when a crowd passed by him, the bastard disappeared.

I couldn't panic. It was possible he saw me, and I was burnt, but I hadn't done anything to draw attention to myself. I'd only locked my eyeballs on him by pure Irish luck, and Nigel wasn't Irish. I folded the newspaper and started to walk toward the ticket counter. It seemed like a natural thing to do. While I stood in line, I caught a glimpse of the tweed jacket and porkpie hat walking toward the platform. I was glad I'd taken the time for a second glance. It wasn't Nigel. It was the kid I'd seen panhandling earlier, wearing the limey's duds. Cute, Nigel, real cute.

I moved up in line and had just gotten to the clerk at the counter when I spotted that gray turtleneck sweater under neatly combed blond hair. Nigel moved like a man with a purpose, and he held a ticket in his hand.

"Monsieur?"

I watched Nigel cross the platform.

"Monsieur?" the clerk repeated.

Nigel boarded train number 176. I had no idea where 176 was going.

"Monsieur!" The clerk demanded.

I snapped my neck back to the clerk. I wasn't there to buy a ticket. So I stepped aside and let the next customer have his turn. I needed to get to a phone.

Fortunately, there wasn't a line at the telephone booth. I grabbed the receiver, plunked a few francs into the slot, dialed, and waited. You have to be careful when using a strange phone. Somebody could always be listening.

"Hello," said Reynardie.

"It's me, I made him. Train 176."

"You're fucking kidding me, son," he replied.

"Nope. Train 176." I looked over my shoulder as the wheels began to move. "It's pulling out of the station now. I'll call you back when I find out where it's going."

"We have a train schedule. Your drinking buddy can translate it. I'll call the French flatfoots and give 'em what we got now. Good work."

The line went click.

I was feeling pretty pleased with myself as I hung up that phone. A big man in a dirty white shirt stood behind me, glaring impatiently. With a shrug, I stepped out of the way as he moved into the phone booth. Turning around, I saw the back of a man in a gray turtleneck sweater with blond hair, boarding a completely different train. My eyes darted to 176, but of course, Nigel wouldn't exactly be sitting by a window with his mug pressed against the glass. The other train was parked behind a larger one, and I couldn't see the damn number. The train started to move. Nuts!

I fast-walked across the platform as the mystery train rolled slowly out of the station. Just before it picked up speed, I grabbed the handrail and sprinted as the train accelerated, and hoisted myself up into a passenger car. It was a near thing, but I was now on the same train as Mr. Gray-turtleneck.

I only hoped it was the right gray turtleneck, or this was going to be more than a little embarrassing.

Pausing for a moment, I collected my breath before stepping inside, entering the passenger car as if it was the most natural thing in the world to board a train already moving. I must've done a fair job of it too because most folks didn't even look up at me. Eyes front, I walked down the aisles of wooden benches that made all European trains feel like churches. My destination; the smaller room in the back of the car that resembled a confessional.

The great thing about a bathroom was that the longer you stayed in one, the more people assumed you must have already left. After a while, they usually forgot who went in there in the first place, and you could emerge a new man, so to speak. I had no way of polishing to change my appearance, but every guy wore a gray suit at one time or another in his life, so I was already pretty anonymous. Then, I heard words that chilled my bones.

"*Billets! Madams et monsieurs, billets!*"

My French wasn't great, but it didn't take a Harvard graduate to figure out who was shouting and what it meant; the damn ticket master, asking for something I just didn't have. This day just kept getting better and better.

I waited and soon heard his voice pass by the latrine door. I opened up and started walking the other direction, but he heard me. Nuts.

"*Monsieur. Monsieur!*"

I turned around to see an elderly guy in an old-fashioned conductor's get up. Well, it would be old-fashioned in the States anyway. I smiled and reached into my pocket, and feigned surprised when I didn't find what I didn't have. Going through all my pockets, I did a mock search for the non-existent ticket. The conductor's face sagged, and his eyes rolled; he'd probably seen performances like this before. Then, I tried his patience in the worst way I knew how. I spoke English.

"My, my, sir, I am so embarrassed. Why this never happened to me before, you see. I was just on my way to this beautiful little town. You know the one with the little red roofs? Mary…that's my fiancée, Mary. She was supposed to meet me, but well, we've had some problems lately. Anyway, I...."

He gave me a look that not only said he didn't speak any English, but he wished to God I'd stop. So, I ended his torture by reaching into my wallet and pulling out an American fiver. "Will this do, sir?"

He snatched the bill from my hand and walked away, shaking his head. Another clueless foreigner in his country, what's a guy to do?

Figuring I'd made enough of a spectacle of myself in that car, I moved to another one and found a place for my butt on one of the hard, flat benches. So far I'd been in two cars on this train, and no rogue MI6 agents in gray turtlenecks yet. Of course, that was hoping that Nigel was still even wearing his sweater…if he was even on this train. I looked around and gave everyone a second glance. Nope, not here.

Waiting a while, I eventually decided to use the bathroom again; only I didn't seem to like the one in that car so went to the next instead. I didn't spot Nigel, but I did spot the sweater, worn by a raven-haired beauty about twenty-five years old, sitting in the middle of the car, right by the emergency exit. She was definitely not the guy I'd seen boarding this train, but it was definitely the same sweater. Trying to swap clothes with a man you don't know is fairly easy, given the right circumstances. Swapping clothes with a woman you don't know is next to impossible. Chances were good that little Miss Raven-hair was an associate of Nigel's. If I couldn't find him, maybe she would do it for me.

    Not wanting to break cover, I went right past her and used the john. Actually, I really needed to go that time anyway. As I stepped out, I took a seat in the front row with my back to her. She could only go so many places on a moving train, and I could only lose her if I spooked her. It was a measured risk. I couldn't see her, but in that position, it looked like I wasn't trying to. It would've been handy if there were a reflecting window or some shiny steel I could watch her in, but nope, not on this antique locomotive. Still, I'd made enough of a spectacle of myself by jumping on the train like Tarzan, having no ticket, and switching cars twice. I figured it was best to lay low for a while and just enjoy the ride...to wherever the hell we were going.

    My stomach started to growl when we reached the outer edges of Paris and entered farm country. We didn't go far. The train made a stop at a little town called Epernay. As the car lurched to a halt, I got up and stretched. Sure enough, Raven-hair reached for a suitcase in the overhead rack. With her back to me, I looked natural enough falling in line behind her. Nigel was nowhere in sight.

    Hanging back among the crowd, I followed her down the platform. She stopped to chat up the conductor, so I stopped and pretended to check a schedule. Nigel chose that moment to slip off the train. He wore an off-white linen shirt and chinos, but no hat to cover his perfect blond hair. When Nigel passed behind the conductor's back and entered the train station, Raven-hair blew the conductor a kiss and went to join him. The couple made a sweet pair as they walked arm in arm through the small, yellow brick station. Always the gentleman, he offered to carry her suitcase.

    Together, they strolled out of the station and into a bistro just across the street. My options were limited. There were no French policemen in sight. I could try to arrest Nigel myself, but I wanted to know who Raven-hair was first. If she was a player, I needed to know whose team she was on. For all I knew, she could be more important than Nigel. Whatever the case, I needed to call my boss before this thing got out of hand. The station had one phone booth just off the lobby.

When I picked up the receiver, the line told me it was dead. I slammed it down in frustration. A little man in a green shirt and cap came up to me and started babbling in French. He said something about a door, and I realized I was standing in front of his broom closet. I couldn't remember the French word for phone, so I gestured with my hands like I was putting one to my ear. He nodded and took me to the stationmaster's office and handed me the telephone. At least that got me out of his way, I supposed.

Then I remembered the French for it, *téléphone*. Boy was I a dolt. I dialed, it rang once, and someone picked up. "It's me again."

"And just where the hell are you?" Reynardie demanded.

"A charming little train station, in a berg called Epernay. The red coat switched trains on me, so I had to tag along."

"Red coat?"

"Yeah," I replied. "As in the guys Paul Revere warned us about."

Reynardie paused. "Oh, got it. You have eyes on?"

"Yes, sir, but he ain't alone. He's got a cute little brunette with him. Mid-twenties, smooth features, maybe five foot six. Her complexion says Spanish, but I don't know."

"Well, son," said Reynardie. "Who the hell is she?"

"No idea."

Reynardie paused at the other end. "Are you in any danger?"

"No."

"Have you been made?"

"I don't think so, Sir."

"Okay, we got an operation as of now. Keep the red coat in sight, but do not engage. I gotta make some calls. When you next contact me, I should have some instructions for you. I'll keep someone by this phone at all hours until this thing is done. Call at least twice a day."

"I copy. Out." As I hung up the phone, I noticed the office window offered a good view of the bistro. I would've preferred a closer look, but I was on my own. If I got burnt the operation was over. Grabbing a paper cup to the water cooler I cleared my pipes. My stomach was growling, but that was too bad for me.

I watched from that window for the next hour. Must have been the stationmaster's day off; nobody bothered me. I kept trying to figure out what would make a guy like Nigel turn Commie. It was true that in this business you could never be one-hundred percent about anybody, but he just didn't seem the type. The Communists who showed up in my neighborhood were all these idealistic young kids. Like missionaries among the cannibals, they'd chat up anybody who'd listen about class, oppression, and stuff like that. They had a passion for politics like most guys have for sports. Nigel never talked about sports or politics, but he did occasionally make a quip about "king and country" as if it meant something to him. Besides, if he hadn't shown up Axis Sally might have given me a lead ulcer, and I owed him for that. I needed to figure this out if anything I knew about Nigel was going to make sense to me.

Good things come to those who wait. Nigel and the mystery broad emerged from the bistro looking well fed and relaxed—jerks. He now wore a tan jacket and a brown fedora. He still carried her suitcase, and I supposed the "gentleman" wasn't going to give it back. As often as Nigel "polished," I was surprised he didn't sparkle.

Raven-hair got into a little black Volkswagen and I got a good look at the license plate when she pulled away. It wasn't a French plate; that I was sure of. I grabbed some stationary and scribbled the number down. Nigel didn't even wave goodbye to the nice lady. He crossed the street and entered the train station. I switched windows and got a glimpse of him strolling onto the platform. He took a seat on a bench, exactly like a man waiting for a train. I learn from my mistakes. I left the office and went to the ticket counter. This time, I paid my fare.

CHAPTER THREE

I boarded the same train car as Nigel. It was risky but as slippery as he was, I couldn't afford to take my eyes off the son-of-a-bitch. Taking a seat in the middle of the car, I sat sideways with my feet to the aisle. Nigel took a seat in the back row, giving him a great view of the entire car. I pulled my hat low over my face to keep him from recognizing me and pretended to take a nap.

Then two gorillas boarded the train and sat to Nigel's left. I swear one looked like Uncle Joe Stalin himself. The guy had that same thick mustache and heavy build. The only difference was that this "Stalin" had horseshoe pattern baldness. The other guy looked like a muscular version of Curly from The Three Stooges. Except this stooge didn't smile. These were serious guys.

They didn't say anything, just exchanged glances with the Brit. It didn't take a super spy to recognize that they knew Nigel and he knew them. I didn't like how this was going but, at that moment, all I could do was feign sleep as the train lurched forward and continued its eastbound journey.

For the next few hours, I grappled with my growling stomach while we passed through French farm country. My neck developed a kink from the hardwood bench, and after a while, I gave up the act of taking a nap. Turning my back to Nigel, I reached into my coat pocket for a cigarette but found my father's letter instead. I opened it.

***

Dear Shawn,
Hope things are going well for you over there. I know Paris must be hell, but I am sure somehow you will manage. Watch those French women. I do not want you bringing anything home you cannot hang on the wall or put on a shelf.

We went to church on Sunday. Father Mike was asking about you. I told him you are fine and the army is treating you okay. He said he would pray for you, but I told him the war is over, nobody is shooting at you, and you are going to be fine.

Son, I got some bad news. I got laid off from the plant last week. They were re-tooling it from war production, but they had some problems. I do not want you to worry. I just do not think keeping stuff from you would help. I will find work soon. In the meantime, I am driving Bugs around. He is not doing the kind of stuff he used to. Bugs has gone legit and is in city politics now. But he still has enemies and having me around makes them want to stay away.

Son, I know you are not crazy about the army, but this is a good time to be a soldier. Things are looking like they might turn around, but jobs are scarce at the moment. If you can do a good job for the army, maybe you can get a government job or something when you get back. I do not want you to have to go through the stuff I have. Be careful over there and tell your buddy, Fred, to buy his own damn cigarettes from now on.

Love, Dad

***

Dad got laid off...nuts. That was all he needed just now. I read the American papers and knew that the war jobs were ending and folks were looking for work. But it wasn't like the depression; I hoped.

For a working stiff like my dad, this was terrible. The man had worked all his life, but no matter how hard he tried, it seemed nobody wanted to keep him. Except for Bugs, and dad didn't like the kind of work Bugs gave him to do.

I'd no idea what kind of job I was going to get when I got home. Maybe I should make a career of the army? I didn't care for the uniforms or the marching, but in counterintelligence, you never really did that kind of thing anyway. Maybe this was my niche? So far I liked the job okay. I still had a few months left on my enlistment and was in no hurry to decide. Folding the letter, I put it back in my pocket.

A quick glance to the rear and there was Nigel, sitting by Curly and Joe, situation normal. As afternoon turned to evening, I got up to use the confessional. Just when I unzipped my fly, the train jerked and crawled to a stop. Wonderful, I thought, just wonderful. People were shouting in French, and I wished for the thousandth time that I spoke more than a few phrases of the damn language. Exiting the latrine, I saw the entire population of the car grabbing their luggage and getting off the train. I tapped an old passenger on the shoulder and asked, "*Pour quoi?*"

My accent must have been very obvious. "You are American, no?"

"Uh, yes," I answered.

"There is a bomb next to the tracks," he said. "We go walk now."

"A bomb? Why the hell is there a bomb by the tracks?"

The old man shrugged. "A farmer found. Maybe first Great War, maybe last one. Who can say? We walk now."

The long summer day came to an end and it was starting to get dark. I got off the train and followed the line of passengers past a farmer and two conductors, who guided us around a half-buried explosive that was probably dropped by my own beloved Army Air Corps just a few years back. While we snaked along a dirt path, I glanced about for my quarry. It took a minute, but near the head of our traveling column, I spotted Nigel and company.

Unfortunately, one of them spotted me too. Shit!

I locked eyeballs just for a second with Uncle Joe before I looked away. I probably turned my head too quickly, because when I casually turned my head back, he was still looking at me. His stare lasted only a second, but I knew he knew. He turned to his fellow gorilla and said something. I was burnt.

There was a village about a mile ahead, and I sure hoped I'd make it. I still had my Colt .45 pistol, but there wasn't a round in the chamber. If the gorillas tried to take me out, I'd need a few seconds to draw it, then lock and load a round. Seconds I may not have.

As the sun sank low, I considered dropping back from the pack and hiding in the bushes. That would be stupid, however, because it would give Nigel's goons the chance to find me and rub me out without any witnesses. I needed room to breathe. Since I was already burnt, I figured it was time to start making friends. The old guy who spoke English seemed like my best shot.

"Excuse me, sir. Do you know what village it is we are walking to?"

He smiled at me, a good sign. "Yes, it is Rathel."

"Do they have a hotel?"

His eyebrows lowered. "A…hotel, sir?"

"Yes, you know, an inn?" Perhaps his English wasn't perfect after all. "A place to rent a room for the night?"

"*Oui*…I mean yes. There is an old family house. I will take you."

While the old man and I continued to walk into Rethel, I made a point of chatting him up for all the crowd to hear. I wanted witnesses to remember me. He was a mechanic returning from a visit with his daughter, who now lived in Paris with her husband and two children. Rethel wasn't his destination though. He lived in the next village over. The old fellow did, however, have friends in town, and he planned on imposing on them for the night. While he and I chatted pleasantly, I lost sight of Nigel and his thugs. Shit, I thought, the perfect end to the perfect day.

When dirt path turned to cobblestone street, we crossed the threshold into the quaint farming village. There wasn't much to it, just a few shops and a gas station. The old mechanic led me to the town's quaint little hotel. I couldn't see any sign that we were followed, but that gave me little comfort. In fact, I would've preferred to have a glimpse of Nigel and company; then I could maybe find a cop or two to help arrest them. Just to know what the score was would even be some small comfort. Not knowing where they were or what they were doing drove me nuts. If they turned the tables on me, I was one against three, and the police might never even find my body.

The old man was very friendly. He even helped me over the language barrier with the hotel clerk. Soon, I held the key to a room in one hand while I waved goodbye to my French buddy with the other.

Then I just stood there wondering what to do next.

Having skipped lunch and dinner, my stomach growled like hell, so I went into the hotel bar and ordered a loaf of bread and some cheese to take to my room. As the bartender wrapped the food in wax paper, I looked around; still no sign of my thuggish friends. Did they even know I was in this hotel? There was no way to be certain.

I saw a public telephone in the corner. Time to check in.

Fred Sands answered the phone. "Shawn, where the hell have you been?"

I was in a public place and wasn't about to take the chance that I was the room's only English speaker. "Good to hear your voice too, Mother."

"What?"

"Listen, Mom, I'm not going to be home tonight. The train had to stop just short of a town called Rethel. Everybody, and I mean everybody, had to get out and walk. I'm afraid I lost your Paris souvenir. You know, that red coat. But don't worry; I don't think it was one of a kind. In fact, I saw two others like it today and they were going as a set."

Sands got annoyed. "Riggs, what the hell are you talking about? Oh, wait, are you in public or something?"

"Yes, Mom." God, I prayed, please let Sands be writing this down. "I love you too. Be sure to tell Dad everything I said. I'll call back first thing in the morning. Bye."

I hung up the phone and went to my room. It was on the top floor of a three-story Tudor building with only one staircase.

Looking around, I confirmed I was alone in the hallway. Drawing my .45, I quietly racked the slide. Locked and loaded, I entered the room, gun up and ready, but there was no welcoming party. Locking the door behind me, I propped a chair against the knob as I slid the deadbolt home. Could Nigel and his goons find out my room number? Did they care? Maybe I was just being scared, or maybe I was being safe. Sweat greased my palms as I put the pistol down on the nightstand and took off my suit.

In all those private-eye movies the bad guys always come bursting into Bogart's room and start shooting up the bed. Deciding to err on the side of caution, I slept on the floor that night, keeping my gun by my side, hammer back and the safety off. Any bruiser that came through that door was going to get it. Shawn Riggs wasn't going down without a fight!

Nothing happened.

I ate the bread and cheese, washing it down with some nasty tasting tap water from the bathroom. Burning my last cigarette in a failed attempt to relax got me nothing. At most, I got two or three hours of sleep that night. Every creak of every board in the hotel sounded like a bat cracking a ball out of Fenway Park. If this was part of the job, I wondered if counterintelligence was really the thing for me after all. Maybe I should have just let the army train me to be a cook, like my cousin Henry, just another draftee.

"Too late now, Shawn, my boy," I said as I closed my eyes for the hundredth time and tried to get some sleep on that hardwood floor.

***

The sun poured in through the window and onto my face. I got up and rubbed my back. It felt as stiff as the boards I'd slept on. The new day gave me a new perspective, and I was beginning to think I'd been a little too paranoid last night. After answering nature's call, I looked at a truly horrible version of myself in the mirror. Naturally, I hadn't brought my shaving kit or comb, so I wasn't going to get prettier any time soon. Well, I figured, breakfast should help anyway.

I opened the door and looked left and right along the empty hallway. No Bolshevik assassin awaited me. Perhaps I wasn't really that important to Europe's fate after all. Fine by me. Truth be told, I felt silly about the whole thing.

The bar served breakfast, and I had an omelet with cheese that went down well. The food revived me, and after my second cup of coffee, I began to feel like myself again. I looked at my watch; eight in the morning, time to check in

"Riggs, what's going on?" Reynardie's voice was a bit anxious but still sounded good to my ears.

"I'm okay, Dad. But I lost my red coat and the two other souvenirs. I'm coming home today."

There was a pause. "Well, it was a long shot anyway, son. I was surprised you even found that coat in the first place. By the way, we ran the plate. The car belongs to one Otto von Kurtz of Frankfort. Know who that might be?"

"Gee, Dad, I never heard of him either," I answered.

"Seems he's an informant for the French Intelligence Service. They haven't seen him for a month, though, and are wondering what happened to him. How about the fem? Did you learn anything more about her?"

I almost forgot about little Miss Raven-Hair. "No, Dad, I wish I did."

"Well, if you do, the high and mighty at G2 sure seems interested. They don't know her either, but she's been popping up in all kinds of interesting situations lately. She may be a Russian who worked in England during the war, but we don't know for sure."

"Well, Dad, I don't think there's much more I can do if I'm heading home. Is there?"

Reynardie sighed. "No, Shawn, I'm afraid not. Fact is, I wouldn't have even sent you to the train station in the first place if we had anything else going on at the office yesterday. It was a one in a million chance from the start. I'll see you when you get back."

I nodded to myself. Nigel and his buddies were a hundred miles away by now. "Sure thing, Dad. See ya' soon."

He chuckled. "Bye, son."

I hung up the phone and shoved my hands into my pockets. The whole thing had been a great, galloping waste of time. But, hey, it got me out of the office for a while. I paid the hotel clerk for my night of blissful comfort and collected the receipt. When I got back to Paris, it would be part of the travel voucher I'd be typing up. This was army business, and I sure didn't feel like paying for it without promise of reimbursement. Heading out the door, I walked into the bright clear morning.

Stepping into the street, the sun caught my eyes and blinded me. I blinked and took a step back, and that fraction of a second turned out to be the difference between being smacked head on or clipped in the side by a small gray car that screamed from out of nowhere.

The car's hood connected with my hip and spun me into the wall of the hotel. My face planted into the timber, and I staggered back to clip the rear fender of the car as it zoomed passed me. My feet went airborne, and my shoulder blades hit the cobblestones with a painful whack.

Through hazy eyes, I got a quick look at the car as it continued on its way…some kind of little French jobber. But I was in no shape to give it so much as a Bronx cheer as it sped out of sight.

Jesus H. Christ, somebody had just tried to kill me!

CHAPTER FOUR

As I lay on the cobblestones, people came rushing around me, babbling in French. They helped me to my feet, and I took stock of the damage. My head bled, my hip and shoulder throbbed with pain, and my pants were torn at the left knee. Otherwise, Mrs. Riggs's little boy was going to be all right.

The good Samaritans of Rethel took me back into the hotel bar and sat me down. Somebody poured me a glass of wine, and I drank it with a sincere, "*Merci.*"

Soon, I was talking to a policeman whose English was only slightly better than my French. I gave him all the details of the "accident" I could, but when he asked my profession, I pretended not to understand.

The cop went on his way, and I finished the wine. I offered to pay, but the bartender wouldn't hear of it. He apologized for the accident as if it was his fault, and wished me a good day. Cautiously, I stepped back into the street. No gray car, no Uncle Joe or Curly Stooge, and no red coat either. With all the attention I'd gotten from the crowd, I doubted if they'd stuck around. But I sure wished they had! My .45 was still cocked, and my trigger finger itched like crazy.

Sons-of-bitches.

I stood there for a few minutes and considered my options. The smart thing to do would be to just get my butt on the next train going west and high tail it back to the office like a good little soldier. But unfortunately, being as young and angry as I was, the smart thing didn't even occur to me. No, my Irish temper was up. I was going to get those bastards; but where to begin?

Looking at my torn pants, I decided the first thing needed was to get a new outfit. I walked around a bit; actually, I limped around a bit, and damn my hip was getting sore. In a while, I found a little shop that sold baby strollers and used clothes. I didn't look at the strollers but picked out some nice twill slacks and a brown and white striped collared shirt. The proprietor only wanted a couple of bucks for the shirt and trousers, and even offered me a discount on a Panama hat and a brown linen jacket—if I would give him my fedora and suit coat. So much for Mom's birthday present, but I had other things on my mind just then.

I asked the guy for directions to the train station, and he told me that there wasn't one in Rethel, it had been blown up by the Nazis, and the government hadn't repaired it yet. But if I would walk just eight kilometers west, I'd find one in the next town over. That wouldn't do. I needed to go east, and the sooner, the better. In my mind, I was chasing the guys who'd tried to run me over, as if I could get right on their heels and run 'em down. Of course, that wasn't the way it was going to be, and I knew it. Where they were heading was anybody's guess, but I knew someone who might be able to clue me in; a certain Otto von Kurtz of Frankfort.

Leaving the store, I headed for the town's only gas station to see if maybe they had a car to rent. The answer was "no," but the owner did have a son who owned a motorcycle. Would the son rent it to me? "No." Would he give me a ride to Frankfort? "Yes, for fifty francs in advance."

So, in my dashing new outfit, I climbed onto the back of an old motorbike, which I could tell by the faded remains of a swastika used to belong to the Wehrmacht. A French kid, no more than fifteen, straddled the thing and kicked it to life.

I'd actually never been on a motorcycle before, and I've carefully arranged my life so that I haven't gotten on one since.

The teenager drove his bike like a bat out of hell. With no intention of putting my arms around the kid's waist, for the next four or five hours, I held on to the bracket at the back of the seat for dear life. Trying to keep the Panama hat on my head proved futile. Somewhere between a vineyard and a dairy farm, it flew off into the clear blue sky. I wanted to ask the kid where he learned to drive but didn't have enough French in my vocabulary to ask the question, and the more I thought about it, the less I wanted to know the answer anyway.

By the time we reached the German border, my ass felt like it wanted to trade me in for a new owner. I dismounted, just glad to put my feet on the ground. There were two colored GIs and a half dozen German police standing next to a barber-poled gate that went across the road, stopping us. A small clapboard shack had a sign on it that told you in three languages to stop and have your passport ready. Lucky for me, I could read one of them. A few French gendarmeries sat on the other side of the road leaning against a police car, reading smutty magazines.

A German cop in a gray uniform and a flat-topped black leather helmet held up his hand as I hobbled over and waved. He greeted me in German. Taking a guess at what he was saying, I reached for my American passport and handed it to him. An eyebrow rose.

He turned to one of the US soldiers. "This man, he one of yours."

The American sergeant approached and asked for my name.

"Shawn Riggs." There was no point in lying to the guy; my passport gave him all the truth he needed.

He tilted his head and gave me a sideways look. "What happened to your face?"

The swelling had gone down, but the scratches remained. "I had an accident this morning."

"What brings you to Germany, Shawn Riggs?" he asked.

I told him, "Business," and hoped he would leave it at that. The last thing I wanted to do was let these guys know I was an agent. I figured it'd be a subject of conversation for the next ten people who came this way, and I'd be burned in no time flat.

"What kind of business?"

My mind went to the gray car that struck me. I answered, "Car insurance."

The soldier laughed, "Car insurance? You don't even have a car yourself, friend."

"One problem at a time, Sergeant," I answered while shaking my head. "One problem at a time."

The sergeant gave a good-natured chuckle and waved to the Germans to open the gate. Just as I figured, you get people to laugh, and they usually stop asking questions.

I looked to my teenage companion, ready to get back on the bike, but he was turning the motorcycle around. "Hey, what gives? *Pour quoi, monsieur?*"

He looked over his shoulder, but the bike still faced the other way. Speaking French faster than I could follow, he yelled at the Germans, shaking his fist. Giving the bike a kick, he put it in gear and as the engine roared to life, the little punk raced back down the road that had brought us. Fifty francs in advance, nuts.

One of the kraut cops approached me. "Stupid. Stupid little shit. He say, he no go Germany. He say, Germany bad. He stupid Frenchman."

"Figures." At least this officer spoke some English, and from the sound of it he'd learned it from the American GIs. I asked him how to get to Frankfort. He told me this road led straight to it, but it was several hours' drive. I smiled and asked, "How long to walk?"

At that point, my countryman came to my aid. "You can get a ride with the nine o'clock convoy," the sergeant piped up. "The Red Ball Express got a regular run-up to Frankfort. We usually just wave 'em through, but I'll stop 'em for you."

"Thanks, that's awfully nice of you, Sergeant...?"

He smiled a big American grin. "Greys. I'm Sergeant Greys, Three Thirty-First Transportation Battalion."

I didn't tell Sergeant Greys that I was a fellow soldier, but I doubt if that would have made any difference. He was just a big friendly guy, happy to meet another American far from home. His buddy fell at the opposite end of the scale and didn't seem to want to talk to me at all. I got the feeling his buddy didn't care much for whites, but oh well.

Grays and I sat in the shack, ate some K-rations, and played cards while we waited for the convoy—rummy, penny a point. It was weird…here we were, two buck-sergeants in the same army. Only Greys was a truck driver from Indianapolis, and I was a spook from Boston. Since we couldn't talk army, we just gabbed about home and sports while we waited for the trucks. It was a long wait. The Red Ballers were late and didn't arrive until after dark. When Greys stopped the trucks, a captain gave him some grief, but he eventually yielded to allow a poor American civilian to ride in the back of a duce-and-a-half. I never got the captain's name, but I'll always remember his face. He was the first black army officer I ever saw. The Three Thirty-First was a Negro unit.

I found myself a clear spot in the truck's bed, on a wooden bench by the crates and parcels. Then, I balled up my linen jacket for a pillow and tried to get some rest. I guess I got some sleep but damned if I can say how much. It was a bumpy ride; the Autobahn still had a lot of potholes and a few craters from that war I'd missed. Too bad for me.

When the truck finally lurched to a halt, I blinked my eyes and rubbed sand out of 'em. Was I sleeping? I wasn't sure. Maybe I'd slept and just dreamed I was getting bounced about in an old rickety green truck.

"Mr. Riggs, sir, we're at Rhein-Main now," said the colored private with the thick Philadelphia accent as he pulled back the truck's canvas canopy.

I blinked. "Where?"

"Rhein-Main Air Base, Mr. Riggs. You know, Frankfort?"

Behind him, the early morning sun shone brightly. I looked at my watch; 0445 hours. Morning had broken, and I felt like it'd fallen smack on my head. "Thanks, Private." I sat up and heard the muscles cracking in my back. "Is there a place I can get breakfast around here?"

The soldier shrugged, "Well, we're all heading to the chow hall, but there's a German dinner about half a mile back that serves American food."

"Thanks."

Army chow or a meal at a restaurant...not a hard decision. I started walking and soon found the place. The building was new. Somebody had tried to make the joint look as American as possible, with pictures of Frank Sinatra and Rita Heyworth hanging on the wall. I figured some German entrepreneur had found a good way to separate a GI's dollar from his wallet. They served sausages and eggs, which I washed down with some honest-to-God coffee. Germany had come a long way in just the last two years. The people were no longer the broken wrecks I'd encountered back in '46 and the Krauts were starting to have something like a normal life again. Yay for democracy, I suppose.

The restaurant didn't have a pay phone, but I didn't particularly want to make a call just yet anyway. Reynardie was going to be pissed for me traveling in the wrong direction and all. So I wasn't going to call him until I got some good news. I did, however, need a phone book. I pantomimed to the waitress until she understood what I wanted. She brought me the very newly printed Frankfort directory—the pages still stuck together from the ink. There were a lot of Kurtz in town but only about a half dozen von Kurtz. Otto lived on Zeil Street, wherever that was. Now I needed a map.

I spent the morning trying to find one, and when I did, the map wasn't too helpful. The US Army had redecorated a whole lot of Frankfort from the air just a few years back, and many of the streets didn't even exist anymore. Fortunately, Zeil was still around. It was a residential neighborhood just by the river, and I found it in only a few hours.

Otto's house was a three-story brick duplex with shattered windows on the top floor. The neighborhood wasn't much to look at, but there was one thing beautiful to my eye. Parked right in front of Mr. von Kurtz's fine abode sat the same black Volkswagen I'd seen at the French bistro.

Bingo.

There were no cafes or similar establishments on the street, so I didn't have a comfortable place to watch the house from. To observe without being observed, I went across the road and made my way to the roof of an apartment building. From that high perch, I had a good view of not only the house but also the entire neighborhood coming and going. Then the waiting began.

I still hated waiting, but this time I was motivated. Yesterday morning someone had tried to kill me, and you don't just get over that kind of thing in a hurry. My shoulder was better, but my hip still throbbed with pain and a quiet rage still burned in a small black part of my soul. I wanted desperately to see that gray car pull up, see Nigel and his two thugs get out. Then I'd get the MPs down here and have the whole lot of 'em thrown in the stockade. But that wasn't to be my fate or theirs. Instead, at half-past seven that evening, Little Miss Raven-hair walked out of the house.

She got in the car, went north, and rounded the corner three blocks up heading east. She'd no luggage, so I hoped she'd be back to the house. Either she was visiting fellow travelers, or she lived in the place. Either way, there was a good chance she'd return. I figured it'd make things easy for me if I just staked out the house.

At least now I had some good news. I walked a few blocks until I found a payphone in the lobby of a hospital. I called collect.

My favorite person in the whole damn world, Ecklan, picked up on the other end. "Hello."

"It's me."

"Riggs, where in the hell are you?" Ecklan demanded.

Did anybody at the office just want to know where I was without involving hell? "Frankfort."

"Frankfort? You're in goddamned Frankfort? As in Germany? What in the name of all that's holy are you doing in Germany?"

I moved the receiver a little farther from my ear. I guess Ecklan figured if Reynardie wasn't there to chew me out, he needed to take up the slack. "I'm working, okay, big shot? I'm following a lead Dad gave me."

"Dad? Oh, right, the chief is 'Dad.' Sands told me. So listen, that makes me your 'big brother,' get it? Now, what lead are you talking about? Mr. Reynardie's been waiting for you for two days now, and he's fucken pissed. He didn't tell me about any lead."

"Well, that just shows that you don't know everything. Doesn't it, big shot?" Sergeant Ecklan only outranked me by a few months seniority, and I was in no mood for his crap. "Listen, tell Dad that I've got eyes on that skirt he was interested in. I'm gonna' find out who she is before I come back. It should only take a few days."

"The hell you say. First Sergeant isn't happy not seeing you at formations, and the chief can only cover your butt so long before you're reported AWOL. True story, you're coming back to Paris now. You hear me, Riggs? Right now!"

I hung up the phone. The day I took orders from that jackass was the day I joined the Yankees fan club. Cooling my temper a bit, I set my mind to what I needed to do next. There weren't many options open to me at that point. There was no reason to call the MPs on the dame yet. If I tried, they'd just ask a whole lot of questions that I couldn't answer. After all, what crime had she committed? Staking out the house would do for a while, but I could only learn so much that way. Reynardie said G2 wanted to know who mystery lady was, but to do that I'd have to get close.

Raven-hair never saw me on the train, as far as I knew, so I figured if I could somehow chat her up I'd get something out of her. If she spoke English that was. But then again, I'd seen her talking with Nigel, so that meant I might not have the language barrier to contend with. My bigger problem was that I didn't have an excuse to talk to her in the first place. Without a cover story, I'd be just some guy off the street to her. So I was stuck.

Never having been a Casanova, I just wasn't sure how boy meets girl.

CHAPTER FIVE

Well, faint heart never won fair lady, but then again, neither did a three-day beard and body odor. I checked my map for a hotel. It was about a two-mile walk to a decent place with room service, but very worth it. I checked in around eleven and took a cold shower before turning in to bed. Hot water would have to wait a few more years for much of Germany.

That night, I got my first good night's sleep since I'd left the barracks in Paris. It was wonderful. I dreamt about cowboys, of all the crazy things. As a kid, I used to love watching the Lone Ranger serials on Saturdays at the ten-cent theater. The masked stranger and his red-Indian companion, riding the west and righting wrongs; for a city kid like me, what was not to love? In my dream, I wore a six gun on my hip, a white hat on my head, and rode a white horse down a dusty trail, desperately looking for something, but I couldn't remember what it was.

The next morning, I used the hotel iron to straighten out my clothes, and went looking for a barber. German is a hard language, but if you make your fingers move like scissors around your hair, folks can generally point you in the right direction. A much-needed shave would have to wait, however, as the barbershop was still closed when I got there. Fortunately, a street vendor sold donuts nearby, and I grabbed a bite while I waited. I also spent some time thinking about how to get myself introduced to Raven-hair without raising her suspicion.

Nothing came to mind.

At ten that morning, the barber shop opened for business. And thank God, the barber sold cigarettes. I'd smoked my last one while waiting to get ambushed by Commie thugs in a small Rethel hotel room a few nights back, and I was starting to get the shakes. Camels weren't my brand, but they were a lot better than most of those funny tasting European cigs. I didn't have any of the old

German marks, but with a big American base in town, the guy didn't think twice about taking dollars.

With a clean shaved mug, I walked out of the barber's feeling like a million bucks. Taking out a Camel, I lit up and took a long drag. While my lungs filled up, my spirits lifted, but I still couldn't think of any new ideas for meeting the dame. So I shrugged and went back to plan A; surveilling her from a rooftop.

Extra donuts in hand, I climbed the apartment stairs back to my perch and renewed the vigil. Of course, I didn't know what I expected to see. Raven-hair might live alone or might just as well have Curly and Joe for roommates, and it was anybody's guess where Nigel was staying. My hope was the same as the day before; to catch them all together. That would be swell. To round up a whole Commie ring in one swoop would sure be a fast way to make staff sergeant, and then Ecklan could go take a long walk off a short pier.

But in the end, I had to settle for one lone conspirator. As I watched the house, it seemed apparent Miss Raven-hair lived alone.

She was not an early riser. I didn't even see a light turn on in a window until afternoon. An hour after that, she left the flat wearing a light blue dress and carrying a small purse. I watched her walk north, turning the corner heading east again. She didn't look my way and I doubted she'd recognize me if she did. Just then, the thing to do was watch and wait until I got the whole picture.

My pack of cigs didn't stand much of a chance, and by late afternoon I was down to my last three. The black car stayed parked in front of the house all day, and there was no sign of its owner, Otto von—what's-his-name? Kurtz? That's right; it was Kurtz.

It was hot up on that roof. The long days of summer were upon us, and I would've taken off my jacket if I weren't wearing the gun. As it was, the shoulder holster got pretty damp that afternoon. After a while, I got bored, went up to the house, and knocked on the door. That was probably a stupid thing to do. I planned to give some flimsy story about being a lost American in need of directions in order to try and find out who else was in that house. But no one answered the door, so nothing came of it. I took a walk around the block to stretch my legs, planning to double back to the apartment building.

Strolling along casually, I started to light my last cigarette when Raven-hair came round the other corner. Nuts! I dropped my lighter. The damn thing went skidding along the sidewalk, and it only took her a step to reach down and pick it up.

Smiling, she held it out to me.

"*Danke*," I said, grateful to whatever saint watched over me and kept me from saying "thanks" in English.

"*Bitte*," she replied.

Turning as gracefully as a ballerina's pirouette, she showed me her back and went into her place, exit stage left. I just stood there like a dope for a moment and then walked down the street. Was I burnt? I didn't think so, but who could tell? If I was, would she call Curly Stooge and Uncle Joe to come finish the job they'd started in Rethel? That would ruin my day. Looking around, I didn't see anybody else on the street. I was safe for the moment. But now that she'd seen me, I definitely needed a change of clothes. Time to polish, old man.

When I got back to my hotel that night, I found a clerk who spoke some English and asked where I could buy some new clothes. The guy smiled and offered me a deal. It seems it's not uncommon for folks to leave their stuff behind at hotels. The management kept the old suitcases in storage, but people hardly ever claimed them. For a few bucks quietly slipped into his mitt, I got a whole new outfit, complete with a shaving kit. The powder blue summer suit was a bit big on me, but not overly much. It came with a gray porkpie cap and a paisley tie that looked pretty snappy. I was glad of the deal. My army pay was starting to run low in my wallet. However, I didn't expect a travel voucher would make them reimburse me while I was gone without the boss's permission. Or as the army calls it, absent without leave.

For the next two days, I stood post on the Zeil Street rooftop. Raven-hair had pretty predictable habits. She got up about noon every day and went out in the early evenings. Her neighbors would wave and share a few words with her as she went about her business. She always got back to her place about midnight.

Each night I'd stare at the telephone in my hotel room. I was in trouble, and I knew it. The chief's last orders to me were to come back to Paris, and every day I spent AWOL I got in deeper and deeper shit with the army. But that fear was also exactly what kept me from calling Chief Reynardie. I figured if I found out something really juicy he'd have to balance that against my absence, and I might get out of this with sergeant stripes still on my sleeve. As things stood, I had nothing to report to the boss, and no reason to expect mercy. So I let it ride.

As the days wore on, I discovered that surveillance was about as exciting as watching cement set. I'd eat my donuts, smoke cigarettes, and read the complimentary American newspaper the hotel maid left on my bed. The New York Times wasn't exactly my hometown favorite, and it was always at least a week out of date, but it would do. The Cleveland Indians were looking good, but the Sox were soaring a little higher in the American League. I figured we were a shoe-in for the World Series and kept my fingers crossed. Too bad I'd no one to bet with. Other news wasn't so great; the Russians were making a big deal about the new German currency the US was about to issue. It seemed the Reds thought it was unfair that our Deutsch-marks were gonna be worth more than their Deutsch-marks. Too bad for them.

The Russians were also messing with the rail and canal routes into Berlin. Red Army troops would let just a few trains and boats into their zone one day, and then let a whole bunch go by the next. Nobody seemed sure if this was a deliberate thing or just another example of bureaucratic incompetence. So far, cars and trucks could still get to Berlin, but only on the one Autobahn from Brunswick. I figured they were just pissed off that we weren't giving them any dough like we did the rest of Europe with the Marshall Plan.

When nature called, I just took a whiz on the rooftop. Of course, other needs had to be addressed more directly. So, when I needed to take a dump, I'd walk two blocks south to the neighborhood beer hall, get a stein of suds, and use their john. It was a nice old place, lucky enough to be spared in the last two world wars and not lacking in local charm. The high arched ceilings, fancy tiled floor, and polished oak furniture made it looked more like a church than a bar. But bar it was, and that was fine by me. They served this great dark beer that gave Guinness a run for its money—not that I'd ever admit that to another Irishman. I made sure to vary my routes to and from the joint and did what I could to avoid attracting attention. On the third day, however, that changed, but for better or worse I couldn't tell.

As I came out of the beer hall men's room with the smell of soap still on my hands, there sat Little Miss Raven-hair—right next to the goddamned cash register.

I had to admit she looked a lot better up close than from a rooftop. She wore a short, pale-green dress with puffed shoulders and a modestly plunging neckline. Her legs were smooth like polished mahogany. Black hair draped over her shoulders to a modest but nice set of knockers, and her eyes smoldered with cinnamon fire.

Damn.

I considered just skipping off, but if I didn't pay for my beer that would arouse suspicion too. On the other hand, maybe this was my golden opportunity. After all, wasn't a bar where boy was supposed to meet girl?

Casually as I could, I went up to the register and handed the bartender a few of the old marks I'd exchanged for at the hotel. His eyebrow raised a bit, as he was used to me paying in dollars, but he let it go. Raven-hair gave me the eye, so I flashed a warm smile and said, "Hi."

She smiled back, "Hello, you American?"

"Is it that obvious?"

She crossed her legs. "Clothes are European, but only Americans say 'hi.' English usually say 'hello.' Have been in Germany long?"

It sounded like idle chitchat, but I didn't like her asking all the questions. "Not too long." I held out my hand. "I'm Ted Williams." It seemed like a good alias; I didn't take her for a Sox fan.

She took it. "Pleased to meet. I am Romana."

"Now, I'm trying to place your accent," I said with a smile. "You don't sound German."

"No, I don't." From her curt reply, I got the feeling there was some issue in that, but I couldn't nail it down just then.

Looking across the cash register, I said to the barman, "Put her beer on my tab." Then back to the pretty lady, "Would you like to find a table?"

Romana lowered her eyes and slowly raised them to me. "Yes."

We took a booth in the back. A single candle in an old wine bottle illuminated the dark corner. She kept her gaze on my eyes, a penetrating glare that brooked no refusal. She was strong and confident, and sexy as hell. We talked for over an hour about nothing in particular. She had the kind of easy-going ways that made a guy feel at peace. I liked her.

She seemed to like me too, even laughing at my jokes.

"Okay, here's another one. A string walks into a bar. The bartender says, 'Hey, we don't serve string here. Get out!' So the string goes outside, twists himself up like a pretzel, and pulls loose his ends. When he walks back in the bartender says, 'Hey, aren't you that string I just threw out of here?' The string answers, 'No, I'm a frayed knot.'"

To that, she let out a giggle, and her beer almost came out of her nose. It was a cute little nose. "You funny man, Ted. Your jokes funny, but not mean. I not like mean men."

I had to agree. "There's far too many of them in the world. I figure I don't need to add to the surplus."

"You make sound like leftover war supply."

"Well," I said. "Hate sort of is, but I didn't fight in the war so I wouldn't know."

She shrugged. "Lucky you."

Lucky you? That sounded like something Nigel would say. Maybe I was getting close to him after all. That would be a great thing, but just being around her made me feel lucky. My mind, it seemed, was on more than just the job, but I flat couldn't figure her out. Her accent wasn't Spanish or Italian, but she could pass for either. Where her accent did come from I had no clue at all. Still, her smile was charming and her little laugh delightful. It took me a while to start asking questions.

"So, you knew I'm American right off the bat, but I can't quite place you. You're not German. You look Spanish, but your accent says Eastern Europe. Are you from Greece?"

Romana shook her head. "I am from everywhere, and nowhere."

Great, I thought, that would sure flesh out my report to the brass at G2.

Eventually, we ordered some dinner. The bartender gave a short chuckle and a shake of his head. He brought us some sauerkraut and half a grilled chicken covered in mushrooms…delicious.

"What brings you Germany, Mr. Williams?"

"Business," I answered. "And please, call me Ted."

"And what business is?"

Deciding to go with the same bullshit I'd been using for days now, I said, "Car insurance. I'm a salesman from Chicago. My boss said if I could open up some new markets in Europe, he'd make me the company's European director. Talk about a ground floor. I figured Frankfort would be a good place to start because of all the American companies working with Rhein-Main Air Base just now."

She smiled. "And what kind of car do you drive? One of those big American Hudsons?"

"Well, yes!" I lied. "I've had it since I was sixteen. But it's back home right now. I couldn't afford to have it shipped over here, of course."

"Of course."

"Would you like to know more about car insurance?"

She shook her head. Either she wasn't interested, or she wasn't buying my bullshit. I just couldn't be sure. Either way, I was glad to be relieved from my fiction writing responsibilities for the moment.

"What do you do?" I asked.

A pause, and then she answered, "As little as possible."

"No job?"

She shrugged. "I have some money. But I know you Americans. You are all doing important things, no?"

Now it was my turn to shrug.

"Very well. You are mystery. I see no ring, so is no Mrs. Williams?"

I smiled. "Not yet."

"Is good." She leaned in and I got a better look at her modest cleavage. "Otherwise you would be a very bad boy, no?"

I took a sip of my beer. "I sometimes break rules," I confessed.

She leaned back in her chair and took a long look at me. Her grin turned feral. "We all do sometimes."

As we finished the meal, Romana said she wanted to help me out with my business. She told me her black Volkswagen didn't have insurance, and she'd be happy to be my first European customer. It seemed her car was parked just a few blocks away and she'd be happy to give me a look at its registration papers so I could copy the information. I didn't refuse.

We walked to her car as the summer sunset, and a soft, cool breeze blew; hand in hand, like a couple of sweethearts on a Saturday night date. I got a look at the black car's papers. Of course, they were in German and meant nothing to me. She translated them and was very nice about it. Then, she asked if I wanted to come in for some coffee.

I said, "Yes."

We went into her house. We didn't have any coffee that night.

***

In fact, we walked right past the kitchen and into her bedroom. I made sure to take off my jacket and the shoulder holster it concealed in one motion and draped it over a chair as we entered her bower.

The bedroom was sparse; just a few pieces of old furniture in an overlarge room with faded blue paint. On top of the dresser were several open suitcases filled with clothes, making me think she didn't plan to stay here for long. A huge bed suitable for some Prussian emperor, or maybe Napoleon and Josephine, dominated the room. The blankets and sheets, however, were old, threadbare, and too small for the bed itself. Somehow, I didn't care.

The angel led me by the hand, and I gladly followed, my heart pounding harder now than on my last army three-hundred yard run. Romana's mood was cool as ice, but her body warm as summer. Guiding my hand up to her shoulder, she rested it by her delicate throat. We kissed, not like lovers in the movies, but deeply and passionately in the European way—with our mouths open. My breath came quick and short.

She pulled back from our embrace and let her green dress slip to the floor. Black lace undergarments set off her olive skin. The sight of her gave me chills, and for a moment, I became paralyzed with delight. Stepping back into me, she undid my shirt and threw it on the bed. I watched it flutter like a white cotton bird, flying toward the pillows. Kneeling before me, she unzipped my trousers and untied my shoes.

I let her take the lead because I honestly had no idea what to do.

Romana took my hand once again, and we walked on our knees to the center of the great bed. We kissed with a desperate passion as if the world would end if we didn't. Then she let me work my way down to her firm, warm bosom. At her will, the bra tumbled off her shoulders and onto the sheets. Cupping her breasts in my trembling hands, I gave them gentle kisses as she stroked my hair. I was lost in paradise. She was every bit the woman I'd ever dreamed I'd know and more. When it came time to enter her, my inexperience showed, but she gently guided my soldier to the front line. I soon found the rhythm, plunging into the beat of my heart. She smiled and moaned in appreciation. My moves were clumsy, and I slipped out for a moment, but she held no grudge as I went back in with renewed vigor. Ecstasy soon overwhelmed me, and I was lost to the sensation. I held her close, grasping at her shoulders, as I reached the top of that mountain, and she sighed pleasantly as we climbed back down together.

I didn't know what to do next. She looked sad for some reason.

"Are you okay?" I asked.

She smiled and said, "Of course."

I began to sit up, but she pulled me back down. "Hold me," she said. "Do not let me go."

So, I put my arm around her. She snuggled up to rest that angelic head on my chest. I couldn't move. She had me in her trap, and I didn't ever want to escape. Somewhere in the night, I fell asleep. Any dreams I may have had couldn't compete with my new reality, and so, were quickly forgotten with the dawn.

I felt love.

***

I awoke before the sun, but Romana beat me out of bed. When I emerged, wearing only my pants, she was already in the kitchen. She stood by the counter in a floral bathrobe, making the coffee we'd skipped last night. She looked up and smiled at me, still looking good, maybe better than before.

"Good morning, handsome."

"Good morning." This was incredible; I still couldn't believe what had happened to me last night. Now I had something to tell the next time I went to confession, but I felt proud rather than ashamed for that. Is that why they're called "deadly sins" I wondered?

And here I was with this woman. Did I know anything about her? Not able to think of a clever conversation starter, I went for the obvious. "You're up early."

She smiled and poured us each a steaming cup. "I always early riser."

"Is that so?" I took a sip. The coffee had a hint of cinnamon in it, just like her. Delicious. "Do you need to be anyplace soon, or should I just leave before your husband finds us?"

Ouch! That was the kind of joke that a woman might not find funny. For a painful second I stood there, composing an apology in my head. But she just giggled and said, "No husband, only occasional friend. I would like to consider you my friend."

A big dopey grin spread across my face. She smiled and lowered her eyes to her coffee cup.

I said, "I think we've gotten rather close already."

She nodded. "Good."

"Your English is great by the way; where did you learn it?" I asked.

"In London during war. I worked with British at Bletchley Park."

The coffee almost shot out of my nose. "Bletchley Park?"

She nodded. "I see you've heard of place. But that is not surprising, no? As an American agent, I am sure you been there, yes?"

A cold sweat chilled me to the core. "No, I haven't."

Damn, I needed to shut the hell up now! There was a silence while I connected the dots. They weren't very far apart. "You went through my clothes and found my badge."

"And your gun." She moved a towel by the coffee pot to reveal my army .45 with the magazine out, and the bullets scattered around it.

Oh, yeah, I was burnt. "You know, I'm signed for that thing. If anything happens to that pistol, it comes out of my pay."

"And are you paid to sleep with unsuspecting women, Mr. American Military Intelligence?"

I shook my head. "That wasn't my plan." Bolting out of my chair, I retreated into the bedroom to gather up my clothes. This operation looked dead as a post, and I would be too when Reynardie got a hold of me.

She followed me into the bedroom. "What was your plan, Shawn?"

My real name, damn. I buttoned up my shirt and looked around for my socks. "That's my business. I'm not even supposed to be here. I mean, I was never here, okay. You get it? I was never here."

"Not supposed to be here? Why? Did not American Secret Service send you here?"

Shoes...where the hell did I put my shoes last night? Damn, I kicked them off by the bed. I went looking under the discarded covers.

"I don't work for the Secret Service. They're way above my class, lady. I'm just a regular Joe, like any other working stiff, okay?" I found the left shoe but not the right. Damn!

Her tone gained a puzzled quality. "You are worker?"

The way she said "worker" had a special emphasis. I stopped looking for the shoe. Maybe I could salvage this thing after all?

"Yes, a worker," I turned on my knee to face her. "Like my father and everyone else in my neighborhood who stood in line for bread, a worker. Now, if you'll help me find my shoe, I'll be out of your life."

I went on with my search. There were some man's loafers next to the bedpost, but they weren't mine. I actually found the right shoe a second later, but I pushed it further under the blankets.

"So, you believe in history?"

My mind raced back to those pamphlets that got passed out when I was a kid. I never actually stood in a bread line or a picket line for that matter. But whenever there was some kind of line, these college boys would come around and pass out handbills and they got around. I tried to remember what they said.

I sat on the bed and faced her while I ran my hands through my hair to wipe away the sweat. "History can only lead to one conclusion."

"And conclusion is?" Her body shifted in the doorway, a hypnotic silhouette even in a bathrobe.

Shaking my head I said, "This is too dangerous to talk about. I don't even know you."

She nodded. "Dangerous indeed, for American agent who isn't supposed to be here. Whose side are you on, Shawn Riggs?"

Good question. How I answered it would determine if this ship sunk or sailed on. Reaching deep, I found an ember of old anger and berthed it into a new flame.

"Not the side of the bastards who put my father out of work. Not the side that uses people up and spits them out when there's no more money to be made. Not the side that throws a man out on the street when he was doing the best job he could and trying to feed his family! Life's hard enough when you're on the bottom. Why should there be a class above that keeps you there?"

She stared at me with hard, cold eyes.

"Why are you not supposed to be here?" she asked.

In my school, kids learned a few basic rules of survival when dealing with nuns armed with rulers. Always hide a lie inside a truth; it helps it go down better. "I'm supposed to be back in my office in Paris, but I need to help a friend, a comrade before they get him."

"A comrade?" Romana tilted her head. "Someone in army with you?"

"It's a special friend." I shrugged. "One who is in danger. His old bosses know where he is going and have a trap waiting for him. They don't mean to leave him alive."

"And who is friend?" she asked.

"No," I answered. "First, who are you? Right now, you know far too much about me. I won't let you get my friend too, Miss Bletchley Park. Are you still British Secret Service? Or were you discharged after the war?"

Her mouth snapped shut, and she turned away from me. When she walked out of the room, I put on my shoes. I took my time. I wanted her to think about it. The paisley tie took a moment to get straight too. As I left the bedroom, I saw her sitting at the kitchen table sipping her coffee. It was probably cold.

My gun was right where she last showed it to me. I scooped the bullets into my pants pocket and put the pistol under my belt.

"Your holster is in silverware drawer."

"Thanks." It was right where she said. Reluctantly, I took another step closer to the front door. She stopped me cold with only a few words. Not so much the words but the quiet desperation behind them.

"I stood in line for bread too."

Pausing before the front doorway, I said, "Did you now?"

"Yes, my mother and father and I. Before the war. Until everybody found work and no more lines. Everybody found work except us Roma. Nazis not approve of gypsies."

My eyebrow shot up. My only experience with gypsies was from watching monster movies as a kid. They were always these quirky characters in wagons that told Lon Chaney how doomed he was just before he became a wolfman. "They hated gypsies too? Why, are you Jewish?"

"No," she replied. "Just different. But we die same as anybody."

I put my holster on the table. "You're an orphan?"

She shrugged. "I have family now. I have comrades. NKVD helped me escape. I trained in Russia for year and then to Britain on mission for party."

"NKVD, the Russian Secret Service?"

"Soviet," she corrected me.

"My mistake. So you may know my friend, Nigel?"

"Maybe, but how I know Nigel knows you?"

I took a seat at the table and wondered where I'd put my coffee cup. "I worked with him in Berlin. I helped him confirm some things, and he taught me the rules of how not to get found out. I'm breaking his rules now if you must know."

"And what rules did Nigel teach you?"

"To be discreet, old man. To be discreet."

She smiled and laughed a short little laugh. "Yes, that is Nigel." Then she looked me in the eye for a long moment. I looked back and did my best to seem absolutely sincere. It must have worked. "Can you tell me of trap? I can get message to him."

Shaking my head regretfully, I said, "No."

She tilted her pretty head and batted her eyes. "You do not trust me?"

"I trust Nigel."

Nodding, she said, "So do I."

"You can take me to him."

Now it was her turn to ask a question. "What makes you so sure?"

Absolutely nothing actually, but sometimes when you start telling lies, you just gotta' keep the momentum going. "He told me about you. Said you were loyal to the people. He gave me your address. I've been watching your house for a few days to be sure you weren't under surveillance. Once I was sure, I meant to ask you for your help. But things got ahead of my plans last night."

"A bit far ahead, no? And you were so discreet few days ago, old man, you dropped your American lighter at my feet."

I cringed. "That was an accident."

"A very clumsy accident, comrade." She wagged her finger at me. "You must be more careful in future."

Comrade? Hallelujah, I was in. Now maybe I could stop lying for a moment and learn something from her.

"So, that's how you found me at the beer hall?"

She nodded. "It was not hard. My neighbors told me where you went."

Ouch, that hurt too. "So you know I'm on my own. The army doesn't know I'm here. I need to warn Nigel and get back to base before I'm classified as a deserter. Can you help?"

She looked into her coffee cup for a long time. "Yes."

"Nigel gave me your address, so I figure you can give me his?"

She nodded and seemed to think it over for a while. I found my coffee cup and drank it down, definitely cold.

Finally, she said, "I will give you his." Her words come as half sigh, half surrender. "He is at farm."

"What farm?"

"One north of Magdeburg on road to Stieglitz," she answered.

"This might come as a great surprise, Romana, but I never heard of those places. Can you give a guy a little more help here?"

She just stared at me.

"Please," I added.

"It is in Soviet Zone."

That could prove a problem. We weren't exactly on good terms with the Ruskies, and things looked like they were getting worse all the time. Still, I could already be too late. Nigel might have spilled the beans on our Eastern European operations by special delivery mail to the god-damned Kremlin by now.

Actually, that was a fairly solid assumption, but was it a reason to quit? Well hell, I'd abandoned reason just before climbing onto a kid's motorcycle back in France. Now didn't feel like the time to tuck in my tail and crawl home. By this point, I knew this operation was either going to make me a hero or a goat. I didn't want to be either, but I couldn't stop playing with innings left in the game.

"How do I get to this farm?"

She lowered her head and held it in her hands for a moment. Rising up, she went for some paper and drew me a map. I took a look and could see this wasn't across the street. I'd have to go about three hundred miles to find a little pencil mark just north of nothing, and east of not much.

Mulling it over, I let my thoughts have voice. "I'll need a car."

She shrugged. "I can give."

That surprised me. "Awfully generous of you."

Romana smiled and shook her head. "Car belongs to dead man. Now, it needs to disappear."

"A dead man?"

She nodded. "Yes. He is dead. He was talking to French capitalists. Now he isn't talking at all."

"Otto?" I asked.

Her eyes got wide. "Who told you about Otto?"

Not having a specific lie prepared, I just said, "A comrade." And she accepted that. Perhaps it reassured her that I really was a card-carrying Commie. Perhaps she wanted very much to be reassured.

Reaching into her purse, she gave me the keys to Otto's black Volkswagen. "I not care what happens to car, but must not come back to west. Understand?"

Feeling a chill as I accepted the dear departed Otto von Kurtz's keys, I choked out, "Will you come with me?"

I was half hopeful and half afraid of her answer.

"No." She shook her head, got up, and put the coffee cups in the sink. Keeping her back to me, she continued, "There is job I must finish in Frankfort. Once is done, I go east. Party needs me for another job there. But I must finish Frankfort job first."

What other job would she do, and what job was she doing now? I had no idea, but since it didn't concern Nigel, I'd have a hard time convincing her I needed to know. In fact, asking might just blow the whole gig right now. She'd confided to me on the hunch that I was a Communist like her. That hunch, however, was only a spark, and I could snuff it out or let it burn by what I said next. The safest thing to say, of course, was nothing.

I let it pass while strapping on my shoulder holster and donning my suit coat.

In a few hesitant steps, I approached the counter to stand beside her. I didn't know what to say, and I didn't know what to do. Casanova must have been a real bastard because I hated using a woman like this. She was so close to me last night when I knew nothing about her. And now, I knew enough to get her arrested or maybe killed, but she was somehow more distant from me than before. Were we still sweethearts? Had we ever been sweethearts?

Light from the morning sun shone through the window and kissed her cheek. She was so beautiful, so tragic, and so dangerous. Suddenly, I couldn't bear to be with her a moment longer. The weight of my lies pushed down on my head like a pile of bricks. Soon it would crush me. Without a word of goodbye, I spun around and quickly marched for the door.

CHAPTER SIX

The black Volkswagen wasn't exactly showroom new. For one thing, the upholstery had an old, musty odor to it. The seats were worn, and a clump of rags kept a certain spring from poking me in the butt. Still, the engine seemed sound, and there was no slip in the gearbox. In fact, it ran smooth as butter.

I'd learned to drive in the army. Bostonians didn't generally bother with cars in my part of town. None of my neighbors could afford one, and there was no place to park a car even if they could. My first driving lesson was in an old Jeep at Fort Devens, and it ended when I plowed into some lieutenant colonel's prized rose bushes. Naturally, I'd improved with practice. I even managed to get my license before going overseas.

Driving down Zeil Street, I turned southwest toward the place where I'd first arrived in Frankfort, the US Air Base. Before I headed east, I figured I needed to stock up on some essentials. But I had to be discreet, old man, as Nigel would say. I didn't know if I'd been officially reported as AWOL just yet. That would depend on Reynardie's ability, and willingness, to stall my first sergeant. The boss seemed to like me. He at least worked to keep Ecklan off my back in our many office squabbles. So I figured there was a chance he'd go to bat for me.

Chief Reynardie had operational control of me, but First Sergeant McGuire handled order and discipline in the company. Even though Reynardie was a warrant officer, McGuire wasn't in his chain of command. The first sergeant answered to Captain Shoemaker, who was on leave when I left Paris. I often heard the joke; military intelligence—a contradiction in terms. The joke always struck me as flat-out hilarious.

I drove the little car to Rhein-Main Air Base and asked the gate guard where the PX could be found.

"Sorry, pal, military personnel only beyond this point. You're going to have to turn that piece of shit around."

I reached into my wallet and pulled out my ration card for the chow hall back at Camp St. Germane. Funny thing, the guard never seemed to notice how my thumb covered my name on the card when he looked at it.

"Sorry, Sergeant. The PX is just past the chapel on your right before you get to the bowling alley."

"Carry on, soldier," I said as I drove on past the self-important little jerk.

Every American base has a post exchange for selling comfort items to the troops. But I wasn't looking for comfort. I needed essentials. I stocked up on some groceries and peanut butter to last a couple of days. Besides that, I picked up cigarettes and two bottles of bourbon. Where I was going, flashing greenbacks would only be a good way to get shot. Cigs and booze, however, were welcome the world over. That was just as well too; when I left the PX my wallet was empty. The last of my army pay had just run out. Too bad for me.

Luckily, some of the best things in life are free; like human gullibility, for instance. Cruising around the base in the late morning sun, I kept my eye on the speedometer and the gas gauge. Getting pulled over by an MP for speeding would ruin my whole day, and there was no way I was going to get to Stieglitz on just a quarter tank. What I needed eventually appeared to my left; a big white, plywood sign announced the entrance to the 862nd Engineer Aviation Battalion's Motor Pool. Turning in, I parked the Volkswagen next to a bulldozer and marched right in the front door of the little prefab office.

Throwing up my badge, I announced, "I'm Special Agent Ecklan, US Army Counterintelligence Corps. Who's the duty sergeant around here?"

A skinny kid in greased coveralls almost dropped a soda pop bottle as he shot out of a swivel chair. The chair rolled back and crashed into some cheap, steel filing cabinets. "Sir, Sergeant Kirks ain't here just now. He went to get some lunch with the rest 'o the fellers."

I looked at my watch, 1054 hours. "Kind of early for lunch, isn't it?"

The kid gave a shrug.

"What's your name, son?"

"Uh, Private Morris, Sir." The kid looked around to confirm there was nobody else he could pass me off to. There wasn't. "Uh, we ain't in any trouble, are we, Sir?"

I grinned an evil little grin. This was almost too easy. "No, son, but I need your help. I'm in pursuit of a Commie spy, who may be on this very base. I can't use my staff car; a Cadillac would be too conspicuous." I thumbed out the door indicating the parking lot. "So I need to get this old German piece of shit up to speed right away."

The kid just stared at me, but I didn't say anything more. It's often best to let assumptions pile up in someone's head until they decide to do what you want them to do. It took only a moment, but it worked. "Sir, I can help you. Just show me the car."

I did.

"It ain't exactly a piece of crap, sir. These German sedans are made real sturdy. Why I hear the seals are so good the dang things will even float."

"Great, son, but I just need it to run on land."

In less than fifteen minutes, the kid filled my tank—exactly like I asked. He also checked the engine (in the back of the car of all places). But he didn't stop there; he checked the air in the tires and even cleaned my windshield. I got to say; I was impressed. Earnestly doing his best, he saw that the little kraut car lacked for nothing. Once finished, I rewarded his efforts by lying to him some more.

"Son, thanks. You did great. Now I got to remind you, this is a secret mission."

His little head bobbed up and down. "Yes, Sir."

"Raise your right hand."

He did so.

"Do you solemnly swear not to reveal anything that just happened today to anybody? National security is at stake, son."

"Yes, Sir. I swear."

I gave him a curt nod and a firm handshake. "You're a fine American, soldier."

Then, I got back in the little black car and drove away. I figured with the oath and all that jive, the kid probably wouldn't tell anybody he saw me for at least an hour, and I'd be long gone by then.

***

Driving north to Brunswick to take the Autobahn east seemed my best bet since that was the only road to Berlin that hadn't been blocked by the Reds yet. However, outside of Stieglitz, Romana's map said I'd have to get off the beaten path to find this farm. That would take some Irish luck because I really didn't have a clear idea of how I was going to get off the main road without getting stopped by the Ruskies. Maybe that was her failsafe? She might have figured that only a genuine Communist would know the password, or whatever, to get through. Of course, I wasn't a genuine Communist, so I had no clear idea how I'd do that. Then again, I didn't have a clear idea of what I would do when I found Nigel, either.

I think the Jewish term for all that was, "oy-vey."

When I got to Brunswick, I pulled off the road just shy of a big red sign in three languages. It read: You are now entering the Soviet Zone. All vehicles must stay on the highway. Be prepared to be stopped and have your vehicle searched at any time.

I put the car in park, made a sandwich, and had a smoke. Back in '46, I'd walked past dozens of Russian checkpoints all over Berlin. They'd just smile and wave as Americans, French, and British soldiers walked around town. Now things were different.

Churchill's "Iron Curtain" had fallen. There'd be no smiling and waving this time.

Reaching into my coat, I found my father's letter. Reading it again reminded me of why I'd started this. Dad always said to do a good job. But I was way past the beginning of this thing now, and I knew it was no longer just about the job. Beyond that, I had no idea what it was about at all. Momentum, maybe? Who knew? I'd stolen second and was heading for third, hoping I'd get home soon after that.

Reaching for my Zippo, I burned Dad's letter to ashes. Whatever happened, I didn't want any of this shit being traced back home. "Well, Shawn, time to screw your courage to the sticking place."

I put the car in gear and merged onto the autobahn.

At least the Autobahn made things easy. Credit where it's due, the Krauts knew how to build a good road. Four lanes of fast freedom with no traffic lights at all. It was nothing like driving in the States. I remember thinking we ought to have roads like that at home, but it would probably never happen.

The car's scratchy little radio picked up the BBC and played some of those corny English songs like "I've got a Lovely Bunch of Coconuts" and "Jolly, Jolly Sixpence." As the mile markers passed me by I kept thinking how glad I was to be from a musical people. Or were they kilometer markers? Oh well, it didn't actualy matter either way. The weather was great, a clear sky on a cool summer day. I rolled down the window and just enjoyed the ride. With no speed limit to slow me down, I figured I'd get to the farmhouse by suppertime.

Then my mind traveled to more sober places. If I arrested Nigel, it'd be easier to drive him to Berlin's American Sector then to turn around and go back to Brunswick or Frankfort. In Berlin, I could find some US Army MPs to throw his butt in a stockade. Then, I'd call Reynardie, let him know that the case was closed, and I could return a hero—or at least maybe avoid that Article Fifteen for going AWOL.

Unfortunately, I couldn't shake this nagging feeling that things wouldn't go down quite that easy. What if Nigel resisted arrest? Could I just shoot him? Of course, I could shoot. I earned a Pistol Expert Badge in basic training. But could I kill him was the real question? Grandpa Dullahan had killed informers back in the old sod during the Rising of '17. But he never said it like it was something to brag about. Had Nigel tried to kill me with that gray car, or had he at least ordered his thugs to do it?

Did that matter?

"Shawn, my boy," I told myself, "you're just going to have to play this one by ear."

I turned off the autobahn east of Kassel and went north on a gravel road. A mile or so in came the inevitable Soviet checkpoint. A Russian truck blocked my way and about a dozen soldiers in brown uniforms stood around toting Tommy-guns. The guy who seemed to be in charge raised his hand for me to stop. I thought that was a good idea. I also thought it was a good time for a smoke, so I lit up a Lucky Strike while I put the Volkswagen into neutral.

My window was already rolled down when "Ivan" came up and started babbling to me in Russian. As bad as my French and German were, my Russian was nonexistent. I only knew one word in their whole damn language; it meant "yes."

I held out my Massachusetts driver's license. Ivan took a good look at it and shook his head and handed it back. He asked me something in Russian, and I replied, "Da."

Nodding, he continued to ask me a few more questions, and to each, I answered, "Da."

After a moment his face grew quizzical. He looked me in the eye and asked another question.

I said, "Da."

Ivan rolled his eyes and turned to his fellows. He shouted something, which they all seemed to think funny as hell. Then he made a gesture as if he was smoking an imaginary cigarette. There are some languages that are truly international, and bribery is one of them. I handed him a carton of smokes.

Ivan just stared at me.

I handed him another carton.

He turned once again to his men and started shouting. They kindly backed the truck out of my way. So, I put the car back in gear and rolled right on past the People's Army with an old-fashioned smile and a wave.

Unfortunately, the Russian Zone lacked anything in the way of street signs, so it didn't take me long to get completely lost on those goddamned country roads, and the next thing I knew I was driving right through downtown Stieglitz.

To be kind, the place was a real shit-hole.

It felt like 1945 all over again; bombed-out buildings, trash on the streets, burned out cars, and people schlepping down the sidewalks like they were half dead. Besides a few Russian military trucks, I might have seen three other cars on the streets, and each looked in worse shape than the last. It was getting dark, but no lights could be seen in the town. The whole place had a creepy feeling, everything broken, everything bad; dogs running wild in the street, the smell of garbage in the air. How long had people lived like this? As soon as I found my bearings, I made a hasty retreat out of that hell-berg, and a town never looked so good in a rearview mirror.

Romana's map was true, even if my sense of direction wasn't. Just as the sun set over the western hills, I found the farmhouse sitting about a hundred feet off a dirt road. The place was more like a deluxe shack than a house, with yellow stucco walls and a roof covered in dead moss.

I drove on down the road for another mile or so and parked the Volkswagen behind some bushes, so it was out of sight from the road. By this time, I was plumb beat and hungry as hell. Reaching into the paper sack, I found more sliced bread and made a quick peanut-butter sandwich. The food revived me while I gave my situation some thought. Tired as I might be, I needed to know who was in that farmhouse.

Just in case, I loaded my pistol.

With the gun in my holster and breadcrumbs on my lapel, I walked back down the road as the stars came out to greet me. One thing was sure; nobody was making a living on this farm. The old barn was slowly falling down, and the field lay unplanted. Young trees surrounded the property, the tallest rising just above my cap. The only farm equipment to be seen was a rusted out tractor that probably hadn't moved in my lifetime. A rose bush grew to the left of the house's front door, crying out to be trimmed, but nobody was listening.

Using the trees and the fading light for cover, I crept in for a closer look. My light blue suit made for piss poor camouflage, but I'd left my fatigues back in a locker on St. Germane a lifetime ago. Inside the house, a few lights flickered in only one room. I figured they used candles or something because there was little chance the civic-minded people of Stieglitz were going to start a rural electrification program around here anytime soon. There weren't even any telephone lines running to the place.

Not daring to get too close, I peered at the lit window from across the yard. The shades were all drawn, but a dim light revealed something from within. Through the candle glow, I could make out three different shadows moving across the window. Who these people were was anybody's guess, but I could be fairly certain they weren't friends of mine. A gray car was parked next to the barn, one of those little French jobbers.

Bingo.

Maybe I could've barged right into the house then and there, gun blazing like a cowboy from the OK Corral. But that would hardly solve my problems with Reynardie and the army. The name of the game in military intelligence is information, and dead people don't tell you much. My job was to catch Nigel, not to kill him.

Also, with the odds at three to one, the chances of ending up dead myself cooled my Irish temper just a bit. So I did the smart thing, for once, and went back to my car to catch some zees. I'd have enough problems come morning, and I figured I could wait 'til then to deal with 'em.

***

With my head pressed against a bunched up suit coat and the cap over my eyes, sleep came to me in fits and starts that night. Maybe it was the neighborhood. The country lacked all of those city noises I was used to. Crickets and frogs tried to sing me a lullaby, but I'd have preferred a cross-town train with the occasional police siren. The country smelled weird too. I figured there must have been a dead animal nearby because I caught a faint whiff of rotting meat. There was just something unnatural about sleeping outdoors.

That's probably why I woke with a start that morning to the sound of a motor—its rhythm stood out against the melodies of nature. I pushed the cap off my face just in time to see that gray car coming up in my rearview mirror. Curly Stooge was out for an early morning drive, all by himself.

Watching the car fade into the distance, I reviewed my options. They weren't all that great. I still didn't have much of a plan, but that hadn't stopped me so far. If I were going to move on the farmhouse, this might be the best chance I'd get. After all, two to one odds were a great improvement over three to one. Double-checking my .45 confirmed it held a round in its chamber and the hammer was cocked and ready. Quickly, I crossed myself in the name of the Father and the Son and took a deep breath.

While the sun peeked up its lazy eye up from the east, I got out of the car and marched on the farmhouse. When I reached the little trees in the front yard, the gun came into my hand, and its safety clicked off. I crouched low and took a good look, but the window shades were still drawn. My heart raced, and my teeth clenched.

I took in a deep breath and whispered to myself, "*Erin go bragh.*"

At a dead sprint, I burst from the trees and crossed the yard to crash into the front door. The old door frame shattered around the latch as the door flew open with a mighty slam. Pistol up and ready, I found myself in a parlor where Nigel sat having his morning tea and toast with the winner of the Soviet dictator look-alike contest.

Nigel's blond hair was perfect.

For a moment, we just stared at each other, their eyes as wide as mine. When I found my voice, It squeaked out, "Nobody move!" Two pairs of eyes blinked at me, but that was all the response I got. I cleared my throat, "Nigel Leer, you're under arrest."

"Am I now?" He glanced at his comrade, then back to me. "You look familiar, but I can't quite place you."

"Special Agent Riggs. We met in Berlin two years ago."

"That American? I thought you rotated home or something. No wonder I couldn't place you back at the train station. My mistake. Do have some tea."

I couldn't believe this asshole, chatting me up like nothing was happening—or covering up while something was happening. Suddenly, a blur filled my left peripheral vision. Uncle Joe was up and moving.

The blast of a gunshot shattered the room as Nigel shouted, "Igor, no!"

The gunshot was mine. Uncle Joe stood before me, unsteady on his feet. He looked down at his chest then back up at me. I heard a clatter of metal on the floor and looked down to see a switchblade knife coming to rest on the tiles. A thump followed the clatter as the thug collapsed by his weapon. There was a hole in the back of his white shirt, a big, red hole.

For a moment Nigel and I just stared at the body. Then my gun rotated to its next target, and I found myself looking at my quarry through pistol sights. He sat perfectly still, teacup in hand. "I'd rather you didn't kill me too, old man."

I took in a few deep breaths. "I'd rather I didn't kill you either."

The Brit turned to his dead comrade. "Well, so much for Igor. Poor bastard."

"He was going to kill me."

Nigel nodded. "Probably so. He'd killed lots of people in his day." Nigel frowned. "That knife has known some uses. Actually, he told me that he killed you in France last week, you know? Said he ran our shadow over with the car."

"My hip still hurts," I answered.

"Your hip?" He took a sip of his tea. "Lucky you."

Nigel was doing too much of the talking. I had to take control. "Put the damn cup down and open your jacket, slowly."

He did as he was told. Opening his gray single-breasted, he showed me two armpits devoid of firearms. "I never carry a gun. That sort of thing tends to give one away."

"You're under arrest, Nigel."

He sighed. "Yes, you did mention that. I suppose the charge is treason, hmm? Espionage against the king? I took you for an Irishman, Special Agent Riggs. Surely you have no love for the British Empire?"

That beat all, an English jerk playing the Republican Brotherhood card on me! "I'm an American, asshole, and I'm doing my job. Now, I haven't got all day. You're coming with me."

Nigel looked at his watch. "You're right. We haven't got all day. In the next hour, perhaps sooner, Peter is expected back from the store. He has a gun by the way, although I'm not sure he's ever used it. Before he gets back, we need to get rid of Igor's body and decide what we're going to do next."

"There is no 'we.' I'm arresting you and taking you to a Berlin stockade."

He shook his head. "You can't do that, old man. I'm on a mission for MI6."

"Bullshit!"

"Agent Riggs, please listen to me." He leaned in toward me, looking down my pistol's barrel straight on. "I'm on assignment. We know that the NKVD has infiltrated the British Intelligence Service. We suspect it's someone very high up. The rotten bastards have been making short work of every operation we've sent east, and not even the Irish get that lucky every time. I was sent by John Masterman himself, to penetrate the Soviet security services as a triple agent."

Oh, hell no, I thought. This was far too convenient for him for it to be true. "And just who is this John Masterman when he's at home?"

"The chief of Twenty Division. He created the double cross system during the war. Used captured German agents to send false reports to Berlin. Worked quite well. So he wants me to play a variation on that theme."

"Pull my other leg, shithead. It's got bells on it."

He looked at his watch again and shook his head. "Please, Riggs. You've got to believe me. I have to complete my mission. Every agent I ran in Eastern Europe has been betrayed from within. I am responsible for those men. Some of them have families! I need to warn them before the Russians start making arrests. Then, I need to keep going east until I can find out who this traitor is from the other side."

I shook my head. "And you expect me to just let you go? You weren't exactly easy to find in the first place you know…old man?"

He closed his eyes. Maybe he was getting tired of the sight of the gun's muzzle in his face. "You know, I saw you at the Paris train station, and a few other times after that as well. Couldn't place the face, but every time I did a check, you were there in that snappy gray suit. Most persistent, I must say. Nevertheless, I didn't betray you. It was Igor who spotted you while we walked from the train to that village." Nigel opened his eyes and looked straight into mine. "I wasn't at all happy when Igor told me he'd ran down our tail. But I couldn't do anything about that after the fact. Don't you understand?"

"And the girl?"

Nigel blinked. "What girl?"

"Romana."

"Oh Lord, does she know who you are?"

I gulped down hard but didn't say a word.

"Bugger it all!" He looked at his watch again. "We have to get out of here before we're both blown. Maybe I can make up a cover story for what happened to Igor, but there isn't much more time!"

"Someone was fouling up a lot of our Berlin operations back in '46. I think it was you."

"Mine were getting botched as well! That's when I contacted Masterman. That's why this mission was planned."

My voice went hard. "And if I still say you're a stinking Commie spy?"

"I'm not," he pleaded.

I said nothing.

"Goddamn it, you bastard! I'm telling you the truth! The lives of every agent I handled are at risk, and I'm playing patty-cake with some fucking American cowboy!"

Honest people always get mad at the end. The guilty get mad at the start and then try to make deals. I lowered the gun and put the safety on. "So, what do we do now, Mr. Leer?"

His chest rose and fell. Silently, he nodded. Lifting his chin up, he fixed me with a cold stare. "We hide Igor's body and get ready to greet Peter when he comes back. And please, call me Nigel."

***

There would be no proper grave for Igor. We simply didn't have time. Nigel took hold of the dead man's feet while I grabbed his shoulders, and we heaved the body off the floor. Igor's half-bald head rocked left and right across my chest as we walked, and my stomach churned with the rhythm. When we got in the barn, I threw up on the corpse.

"First kill, old man?"

I nodded as we dropped Igor behind some moldy hay bales.

Nigel seemed to understand. "Never a sport, killing men. I did my share back in the war. Number Four Commandos, you know? Used to kill German sentries with a dagger across the throat. Didn't like it much. They kicked and made a terrible fuss."

Again, I nodded. What was there to say? I'd cooked a meal of vengeance and found the taste bitter in my mouth. Wrath—was it number six or number two on that list of seven? Would I ever have the courage to admit what I had done in confession? Deadly sins indeed; I'd never realized how well titled that list was. Nigel scooped hay from the trough with a pitchfork until Igor disappeared under it. I felt a little better then.

Better when I couldn't see him.

Nigel put the pitchfork away and looked at his watch again. "Now, I'm afraid we need to kill Peter."

"What?"

"We can't leave him alive, Riggs. He'll report Igor's disappearance, and soon we'll have the whole Red Army chasing us across the countryside."

My jaw went slack. I hadn't thought of that, but it was so damn obvious. Our problems were having puppies. "We kill him, won't he be missed too?"

Nigel shook his head. "Peter alone would report us, yes. Igor and Peter missing will alert no one—right away. They're both NKVD men who were to travel to London as sleeper agents. After they got me safely into the Russian Zone, I was giving them instruction on some of the finer points of acting British before they departed for their mission. It will be assumed that I finished my tutelage and they went on their way. With that assumption in play, I can safely travel east as the agent I am believed to be. But that only works with Peter dead, old man."

"Curly Stooge."

"I beg your pardon?"

I shrugged. "Never mind. How do you think we should do this?"

"Well, it's quite simple really. I'll sit in the parlor and have some more tea while you stand behind the door. We'll leave it slightly ajar so that he doesn't notice the latch is broken right away. He will walk in and see what he expects to see, namely me. As soon as he steps past the threshold, I suggest you shoot him in the back of the head."

I nodded. "Simple."

"And do angle the gun slightly upward when you do it," he added. "Shame if the bullet went through his head and hit me."

He was prepared to betray Peter so easily. Did that mean he was on the level or did it mean that he could just as easily betray me? His actions and his story matched up. I believed him, but didn't know if I could trust him; either way, I still had a gun, and he didn't. I figured I'd keep it that way.

We didn't say a word as Nigel, and I walked back to the house. He threw a rug over the puddle of blood in the middle of the parlor. Igor's knife was tossed into the rose bushes outside the big window. Nigel poured some tea into two cups and offered me one.

"Thanks." My throat was dry. Since Peter could arrive at any moment, I gulped it down in one go. The liquor hit me like a slap in the face.

Nigel smiled. "Nothing like a little nip first thing in the morning, hmm?"

"You always have booze with your breakfast, Nigel?"

He sighed. "I have booze whenever I can, old man. Ever since the war."

The rhythm of a motor intruded on our conversation. I put the teacup down and took my post behind the door. Carefully, I drew my pistol and made sure the safety was off while Nigel poured a fresh cup of tea as if nothing strange was happening at all.

I always hated waiting. This wouldn't be a long one, but it was the worst in my life. Just outside was a man named Peter, returning from a simple errand. I could hear his car's engine die, its door open and shut. Did Peter have a family? Did I want to know? Hell, I didn't even want to know his name, and I already did.

I knew Igor's and I knew Peter's.

I stopped breathing.

Footsteps approached the house, slowly, lazily, old shoes that squeaked. Nigel crossed his legs at the table, blew into his tea, and looked up. The door creaked slightly as the big man opened and walked past it. I saw his big round head.

He said, "Nigel, don't people close their doors in England? I was just—"

I felt the steel trigger press into my finger as if the gun was shooting me, not the other way around. A loud bark shattered the room for the second time in as many hours. Then I heard another thud as Peter's body hit the floor and a crash as milk bottles shattered on the tiles. He fell on the rug that covered Igor's blood; Peter's now oozing into the weave, not from the little hole in the back of his head, but from the gaping maw where his face used to be.

I hated my fucking job.

CHAPTER SEVEN

Staring at the body didn't make it any less dead. I turned my gaze up to Nigel. "Give me a hand, won't you."

Silently, he rose as we gave the same funerary rights to Peter as we had for Igor. This time I didn't puke; my stomach was already empty. Once the hay covered Curly Stooge…Peter—his name was Peter—Nigel and I retired to the house to have another teacup of gin.

"Boodles is the best gin from here to China." Nigel smacked his lips. "I will miss it so. Nothing but vodka from here on out, I suppose."

I took another sip. The stuff tasted like aftershave, but it wasn't worse than the bad taste already in my mouth. "What's next?"

He looked in his cup. It was empty, but I guess he decided he'd had enough breakfast for one day. The teacup went to rest on the table. "We part ways, Shawn. I need to make a show at a spot in the east soon to meet my contact. The meet was arranged before I left London and can't be changed now. I'm to meet with an NKVD agent a bit later who's taking me the rest of the way east. You, my American friend, need to depart my company long before that happens."

"I suppose there's no time like the present. I'm overdue with the army as it is." I finished the gin. "Time I headed back."

"How did you get here in the first place?" he asked. "There is hardly a train station nearby."

I shrugged. "Romana gave me a car. Said it had to go east and not come back."

"Had to go east and not come back? That's a rather strange request, don't you think?"

Again, I shrugged. What was there for me to say?

We took a walk to the Volkswagen, and he gave it the once over. The dirt roads had done a number on its black gloss coat, now dulled by gray dust.

Nigel appraised it. "Looks like a fine little motorcar. I wonder what's in the boot?"

"The boot?" I asked. "There's no boots in the car."

He sighed. "The trunk, old man. What's in the trunk?"

"Don't know," I answered. "I never thought to look."

Nigel rounded the front of the weird little German auto and opened the hood. Taking a quick step back, he declared, "Oh, my," as his nose wrinkled and he switched to breathing through his mouth. Walking around the car, I smelled the same smell and saw the same thing.

"Holy Mary, mother of God."

"Was he a friend of yours?" Nigel asked.

Looking at the body curled up in the trunk, I shook my head. "Never saw him before in my life."

The dead man wore a black suit and argyle socks with no shoes. The skin was pale, the body stiff, and there was a lateral cut across the throat caked in dried blood. Nigel reached in the black suit's pocket and produced a brown leather wallet. As he read the deceased's name, I muttered along without having to see it, "Otto von Kurtz."

"Just an acquaintance then?" Nigel asked.

"Not even that," I replied. "He was an informant for the French, I'm told. Romana said he was dead, but she skipped the part about how he was in the damn trunk."

Nigel paused in thought for a moment. "Hasn't been dead long. I'd say he met his maker only a day or two ago. Did you encounter any checkpoints coming into the Russian Zone?"

"Yes."

"Didn't they search your car, old man?"

"No, I bribed my way through."

"I see. Well, looks like that barn's going to get a bit more crowded, hmm." Nigel shut the hood. "Let's save ourselves some steps and drive him there, all right?"

"Sure." Goddamnit, this day—hell, this week—just kept getting better and better.

We drove the little black hearse into the barn and lifted poor Otto out on a ratty tarp. He took his place next to his fellow corpses with his own blanket of hay to sleep under. Nigel turned and walked away, but I stood by the graves for a moment. Glancing over my shoulder confirmed that Nigel had no interest in the view of my back. I crossed myself and mumbled a quick Hail Mary, then lit a Lucky Strike and joined Nigel in the house.

The Brit was packing his suitcase when I found him in the bedroom. "Tough day, old man."

"No shit," I growled.

He looked up and saw my smoke. "Can you spare a fag?"

"What?"

He shook his head in despair. "A cigarette, Shawn." I handed him one and gave him a light. "There's a good man. If you see me in Berlin, you don't know me, right?"

"Right. But be careful, Nigel. They're looking for you."

He smiled. "But I'm not me." Nigel reached into his barest pocket and produced three different passports—one American, one German, and one Czech. "I am whoever I need to be to get where I'm going."

That gave me a chuckle. Always the pro, Nigel covered all the angles. We stepped out into the late morning air. It was still cool, but I knew that wouldn't last. Nigel and I still didn't have much to say to each other. We weren't exactly friends, but we were no longer enemies. So what were we? He finished the cigarette and snuffed it out on the hood of my car.

"Come with me, Shawn. I have something that might help you on your way."

He turned and walked back to the barn, not my favorite place to be. In fact, it was a good place for an ambush if Nigel decided to end our friendship permanently. Still, he had no gun. No gun that I knew of. Did that make me as safe as I first thought? Could I trust him not to slit my throat with a dagger while I kicked and made an awful fuss?

I let him lead me, and made sure to stay a few steps behind him as we strolled into the barn. He turned right and opened a musty wooden crate. I let my fingertips dance on the handle of my .45 as it rested in my shoulder holster. He bent down and reached into the crate.

"Here they are, then." Nigel brought out three gas cans. "Might as well see this petrol put to good use, hmm."

My hand left the gun and went to wipe my brow. I'll admit, I was sweating. He gave me the jerry-cans and helped me fill the Volkswagen's tank, at least halfway. We shook hands and parted. He drove off first in the little gray car, and I was to leave an hour later to avoid suspicion. Besides, I hadn't had any breakfast, and the food in the farmhouse's ice box would have just gone to waste anyway.

***

After a quick shave and a change of shirt, I started up the little black car. It still smelled so I splashed the last of Nigel's fine gin into the trunk. That helped a bit. "Time for old Shawn to get the hell out of here," I said as my foot came off the clutch and the farmhouse became just an image in my rearview mirror. The sun was bright in the sky and I knew the way ahead. Just a few miles of country road and I'd be on the autobahn to Berlin. Thank God this was over.

Letting Nigel go would be tough to explain, however. Try as I might, I couldn't see how this could end in any other way than an Article Fifteen in my file. Whatever happened, I couldn't tell anybody about Nigel's mission. If this spy was so highly placed in British Intelligence, he would be able to read American reports, and that would be lights out for Nigel. Disciplinary action was a foregone conclusion at this point. Too bad for me.

Oh well, I'd been a private before.

I turned on the radio for some pleasant distraction, but that didn't work. Well to be clear, the radio worked fine. It was the pleasant distraction part that was lacking.

"...Mayor Rotier has called the city council into emergency session. Sir Brian Robertson of the Royal High Command has stated that Britain will stand firm against this treacherous act by the Soviet Union. The American response is not known at this time. As the red noose tightens, the free people of the world pause to consider the implications of Stalin's actions. We will be continuing our coverage of the Soviet blockade of Berlin as further developments come in.

Now to sport, where Manchester United is...."

I never cared less for sports or hungered more for real news in my life. Thankfully, the BBC did continue the story. As my luck would have it, Stalin decided this was the day he'd put the hammer down on all routes leading into Berlin. A total blockade of the city meant to drive the Yanks, Brits, and frogs from town and put the east part of Germany under complete Communist control. Shit.

Romana's map was suddenly useless to me. It only showed the route from the autobahn to the farm and vice versa. Any moron could 'a told me that the Autobahn would now be off limits. So I turned the little car around and started looking for country roads that headed east.

The sun would have to be my compass, and I only hoped I wouldn't have to pull over and ask for directions—even if I spoke enough scraps of German to be able to ask the question, I wouldn't understand the answer. Maybe it was just the Autobahn that got cut off, and the Reds would leave the rural routes alone? Yeah, and maybe pigs would learn to fly after all.

After driving around for two hours in God's country, I learned the score as I fell in line behind a lot of stopped trucks and vans. They'd waited on the road so long the drivers had all shut off their engines and were just milling around talking to each other and smoking. Craning my neck around the traffic jam, I saw the reason. A Russian halftrack blocked the road, and maybe a half dozen Red troopers sat behind a couple of machine guns. No point in waiting around; I put it in reverse and slipped away as quietly as I could.

For the next seven hours, I repeated that performance. I'd drive around, get lost on some God-forsaken dirt road, and then find myself blocked by more Russian troops. As I sped away from one checkpoint, I looked in the rearview mirror to see a soldier jump in a Jeep to chase after me. Fortunately, one of his buddies pulled him out. I guess I just wasn't worth the bother to 'em. That suited me fine.

The radio only helped me so much. The BBC gave the big picture, but I had no idea about the little one that vexed me at every false turn. Dirt roads, traffic jams, Russian troops again, and again, and again, all the livelong day. Finally, I turned a corner into a forest just a few miles north of Berlin; no traffic jam waited for me, and this time the troops were American!

I swear to God I'd never been happier to see dog-faces in my life. About twenty GIs stood around a bunch of Jeeps with .30 caliber machine guns mounted on the tops. Each man wore the flaming sword and rainbow patch of the Berlin Brigade on his arm. I felt like I'd just slid into home and heard the umpire shout, "Safe." My grin was so wide my face hurt as I pulled up and showed my passport.

"Howdy, sir," said the platoon sergeant with a hillbilly accent. "Welcome to Berlin."

"Thanks, Sarge, I'm just glad to see you guys and not the Ruskies."

The sergeant smiled and scratched his face. "Well, there were about half a dozen of those fellers here a 'bouts a few hours ago. Seemed real nervous when we showed up and started cocking our weapons. I think they ran home to tell their pa about us. Can't say how long we can keep this road open. But we're a trying."

He returned my passport, and I said, "Thanks."

"You're welcome. At least you gave me a real passport. I can't see any problem. Now, you just drive straight on until—"

A real passport? I interrupted him. "Sergeant, has anybody tried to show you a fake passport today?"

He smiled a big toothless grin. "Well, sir, as a matter of fact, yes. We had this piece of shit, called himself David Lane. He shows me this US passport and starts talking to me like he's from Virginia, or maybe Alabama. You see, that's the thing; his accent was all over the place. So I get to asking him where in America he's from, and he says Georgia. Well, there ain't no way the sum'bitch is from Georgia, 'cause my wife's from Georgia, and she don't talk like that. Anyway, we call up on the radio and HQ says this feller is on a list. Says his name ain't David Lane at all, but he's some kind 'a Commie spy. So we took him up to our stockade to rest a spell. Dumb shit. If he can't talk American he needs to learn him some English."

"That's great, Sergeant. You've got a good eye."

He smiled a bit wider. "And a good ear, sir. If you don't mind me saying."

I nodded. "And a good ear."

"Ain't nothin." He shrugged.

"No, it's quite a thing. I bet that guy could've slipped past a hundred other soldiers, but not you, Sergeant...."

"Terry, Max Terry."

I reached out to shake his hand. "You're doing a great job, Sergeant Terry."

"Thank ya', Mister."

In fact, he was doing too great a job.

Damn.

Pulling away from the sergeant and his platoon, I glanced at the bumper of one of those Jeeps. In standard army white stencil, it read, *M/2-6 INF*.

Driving south to Berlin all kinds of thoughts ran through my head. Nigel had made a fatal error thinking southern meant stupid. I wondered if perhaps his boss at MI6 could get him out of this, and the answer was probably yes. But doing that would alert whatever traitor was within the British Secret Service, and that would be all she wrote. Nigel would be completely blown and have no chance of warning his network or penetrating the NKVD for that matter.

The dirt road turned to gravel as the trees started thinning out. I'd let Nigel go because I believed him. Bringing him in might have washed all my sins away as far as Reynardie and the army was concerned, but I'd chucked all that. Nigel's actions matched his story, and he didn't betray me. In fact, he let his two companions die to protect me. You can never be one-hundred percent about anybody in this business, but my gut told me I'd made the right decision. Now, the great "Commie spy" had been captured, but someone else would be the hero, and I'd be the goat. And every agent Nigel ran in Eastern Europe would be as good as dead.

I passed some more American soldiers. They smiled and waved. I honked my horn and waved back. The gravel road turned to pavement and the trees to bushes. How much trouble was I in now? I'd been on my own for about a week, so at worst I was still just absent without leave. They didn't call it desertion until after you'd been away a month. Or was it more? What was the penalty for desertion anyway? Maybe a few months in the stockade? After all, this didn't count as a "time of war," so the penalties had to be lighter. Right?

Right, and was it right that people should die just because some dumb-assed Brit couldn't fake an American accent? People who had families.

I rounded a bend and got a good look at Berlin from the north. A lot had changed since 1946. There were a whole bunch of new buildings, and many of the ruins I'd known had been demolished. Oddly, no lights could be seen as twilight fell over the city. That was weird. But it wasn't like Stieglitz. People walked down the sidewalks in good clothes with full shopping bags in their mitts—lots of shopping bags. They seemed worried. Many of those bags overflowed with food. They obviously knew about the blockade and were stocking up on essentials.

Pulling over, I got out of the car for a stretch and lit a cigarette. My knees cracked and my back too. It'd been a long car ride and road weary didn't begin to describe my condition. Leaning against the Volkswagen, I took the time to enjoy that smoke, letting each puff slowly fill my lungs and then flow back out with a long, slow exhale, which turned into a cough. I thought, maybe I should switch to menthols; at least they'd be good for my health. Enjoying the cig to the bitter end, I finally snuffed it out on the hood of my car.

As the evening air blew cool in my face, I made my decision. My boyhood fantasies were about to come true. Now, I was the Lone Ranger. And I was going to bust my Red companion out of jail.

CHAPTER EIGHT

Driving into downtown Berlin, I dogged around until I came to the Zehlendorf District. I managed to get lost a couple of times until I found Saargemuender Street, and rode it all the way to my old office buildings at General Clay's HQ. By the time I got there, it was almost ten at night, and it'd already been one long and lousy day. I took the Volkswagen up another block and pulled over. Checking the gas gauge wasn't too encouraging. I had about an eighth of a tank left and not so much as a dime in my pocket. At least my groceries hadn't run out; one and a half loaves of bread, a half jar of peanut butter, two apples, a half carton of Lucky Strikes, and two bottles of bourbon. It would have to do.

That evening my dinner tasted exactly like the night before, and the same rumpled up jacket again became my pillow. I did, however, sleep a hell of a lot better. Maybe it was the exhaustion, the lack of bullfrogs—or maybe the lack of a dead man stinking up my trunk. But I slept like a rock, and I needed my beauty rest; tomorrow was already shaping up to be another long, lousy day.

***

German is a harsh language. Unlike the French, who treat words like rich butter, the Germans tend to growl out their speech in harsh syllables. When the language is put through a megaphone, it's like taking a cheese grater to your ears. Not the best way to wake up in the morning.

A large black van slowly rolled down the street. On its roof were these big loudspeakers announcing something very important everybody needed to know. Everybody who spoke German, that was. To me, it just sounded like an old man complaining at a restaurant that his bratwurst had gone cold. Then I remembered the blockade. No traffic in or out of Berlin, by order of Joseph Stalin himself. We were all prisoners now, trapped behind Churchill's iron curtain. Nigel even more so as he now warmed a bench in an army stockade. I had work to do.

I got out of the car, took another good stretch, and gulped in a great breath of air as my eyes blinked out the sand. Looking left and right revealed no one sharing the sidewalk with me. Why not? I unzipped and took a leak.

The next thing I needed to get my hands on was some stationary and a typewriter.

Shoving the shaving kit in my pocket, I headed down the street and marched right up to the guard outside the cluster of old Luftwaffe buildings. I didn't even pretend to have a pass. "Soldier! What in the Sam Hill is going on around here?"

The guard blinked his eyes open and gave me the "I wasn't sleeping—honestly, sir" look. Then he asked me the first question that came into his foggy little mind. "What?"

"That's what I'm asking you, Soldier." I regarded him with a sideways glance. "What state are you from?"

"Uh, California, sir."

"Well, I represent Congressman Heselton's office, from the great state of Massachusetts. Now, Soldier, I want you to know that we have everything under control. Yes, sir. Those red bastards ain't going to lick us!"

"No, sir."

"Good man. Now, tell me how to get to the conference room."

The guard blinked. "What conference room, sir?"

"Damn it, Soldier! General Clay is holding a political briefing in"—I checked my watch—"ten minutes, and you don't know where the conference room is?"

"Uh, I don't get invited to too many conferences, sir."

"Oh, never mind. I'll find it myself."

And with that, I walked right past security and into the US Army's Berlin Headquarters. Sometimes I amazed even myself.

The next part was even easier. This place had been my old stomping grounds two years ago, and I knew it like the back of my hand. After a quick trip to the restroom to shave and freshen up, I went to find a phone. Against the left wall of the main hall stood a bank of telephones in a neat row with directories by their sides. Most were in use. The place was going nuts with people hustling around and shouting orders. Good thing one phone was still available. Picking up the directory, I looked for my old office number, but it wasn't in the book. Giving it a quick dial gave me all the information I needed as a wicked grin spread across my face. Then, I looked up the 6th Infantry's Regimental stockade. The number was easy to find and it included the extensions for First Sergeant William Doublemaker and a Captain James Thompson…too easy.

I called the number.

"Stockade, Corporal Witherspoon speaking."

"Yes, I need to speak with Captain Thompson," I said.

"Sorry, sir. He rotated home two months ago. Captain Padalecki is our commander now."

"No kidding. Is that John Padalecki, from Brooklyn?"

There was a pause. "No, sir. It's Mike Padalecki. I don't know where he's from."

"No problem, Corporal. I'll call some other time." Click, and I was off the phone.

Next stop, the typing pool.

It was a series of connected rooms in the back of the building where about forty women sat pecking away. Some wore Women's Army Corps uniforms, but most were in civilian clothes. I figured my chances of getting what I wanted were better with someone younger and less experienced with bullshit artists, so I picked a young one.

"Excuse me, Miss?"

Her eyes left the handwritten notes she was transcribing. "Yes?"

"I was wondering if you could help me. Is there a typewriter I can borrow?"

She let out a heavy sigh. "Just put your notes in the 'in' box at the front counter and fill out an order slip, sir. We'll get to you in turn." Her eyes darted back to her work.

"No, Miss, thank you. I can type it myself." I gestured to the office at large. "Everyone is crazy busy, I know, with the blockade and all. I don't want to be any trouble."

She looked at me with an expression of relief. I wasn't just some other jerk who was out to make her life harder for the sake of it. Instead, I was a gentleman trying to lighten her load. She didn't even ask me who I was or why I wanted a typewriter. "We have an old Underwood in the closet I can get for you. But I warn you, it has an 'h' that sticks."

I smiled. "That will do fine. Thank you, Miss. Can I also have some stationary, please?"

I took a moment to write some notes before I got typing: *Sergeant First Class Terry, M Company, 2nd Battalion, 6th Infantry Regiment, Nigel Leer aka David Lane*. It took me only three drafts, and I had a respectable looking document on official army stationary. The heading read: Top *Secret//No Foreign//Cpt. M. Padalecki Eyes Only, Office of General Lucius Clay, Berlin*. A quick squiggle with a pen and it even had the standard issue, illegible, army officer's signature. I found an envelope and neatly folded it in.

Next, I needed to discover the whereabouts of the 6th Infantry. Happily, that part was also easy. Some go-getter had put up a map in the main hall with the location of every American facility in Berlin. Turned out, the boys of the 6th were some of the luckiest bastards in town. A brand new barracks complex had been built specially for 'em on the southeast side of Krautville. I borrowed a pencil and paper from the corporal at the front desk and jotted down directions to the McNair Army Barracks on Osteweg Street.

Bingo.

***

When I came in sight of McNair Barracks my little car was sucking the last fumes out of its tank. The needle was deep in the "E," and I simply had to hope I had enough gas to get me around the corner once I sprung Nigel. The place was a sprawling complex of white brick buildings, complete with sports fields and a four-story clock tower. The time was 1330 hours.

Troops were going berserk all over the place. Trucks streamed out into the street filled with soldiers, and everybody was armed to the teeth. I had to grab a private by the arm so I could stop him long enough to ask where they kept the stockade. He didn't know but his buddy did, and I made sure I got the information before I let the guy go.

The stockade was a one-story box of a building made of the same white brick as the rest of the place, graced with a motor pool to one side and a football field on the other. Narrow, bars-covered windows faced the street, and it had only one door. A simple sign announced: 6th INF, Special Troops Battalion, Military Police Stockade.

I took a breath, "Next batter up, Shawn Riggs."

Walking in, I was greeted by the usual army set up of a front desk with a duty sergeant behind it and a small office section beyond. The sergeant wasn't in charge, however; chaos was. I watched MPs rushing about with anxious faces and papers in their hands. A beleaguered officer was the unlucky recipient of many of those papers, and he never seemed happy when he got handed one. Everybody wore a .45 on their hip and a helmet on their head.

A rack of rifles, carbines, and such lined the left wall, and a kid by the right wall sat by an oversized radio. The cells, presumably, were behind the coffee maker in the back of the room.

Without making any kind of grand entrance, I sauntered up to the desk sergeant, who was ass deep in paperwork. I leaned in close. His pen stopped moving. "Can I help you?"

I answered in a hushed voice. "Yes, you can, Sergeant. I need to speak to your commander, right now."

He blinked. "Sir?"

"Just get me your CO, okay?"

"Uh, okay." He turned his head. "Captain Padalecki, this man wants to see you, Sir."

The officer looked up from his papers with an expression that screamed, "Now what?" A big man with a chest like a barrel, he lumbered up from his desk and came across the room to meet me in a few, powerful strides. "Yes, Jones. What does he want?"

"I don't know." The sergeant turned back to me. "What do you want?"

I withdrew the badge from my coat pocket slowly, like I was handling something that might explode. "I'm a Special Agent with the US Army Counterintelligence Corps. I have orders to take custody of a prisoner." With my other hand, I produced the envelope and carefully handed it to the captain.

He read it twice, then looked up. "Why does General Clay want to speak to the prisoner personally?"

'You read the order?" I asked.

"Yes."

"Then that's all you need to know."

The captain mulled it over. This was obviously something outside of his routine and deserved consideration. "Why isn't this coming down the chain of command?"

I shrugged. "I'm not in the business of second-guessing four-star generals, Captain. But the Counterintelligence Corps is outside of the normal chain of command. Feel free to look it up in the regs."

"I don't have to." He frowned. "You ain't the first guy to come into an MP station with one of those funny War Department badges since I've been in the army."

"Sir," a corporal from the back shouted as he put down a radio. "First Platoon says they got shooting in the marketplace!"

The captain whipped around. "What? Who the hell is shooting at who?"

The corporal put his ear back to the radio. "Oh, looting. Sir, they said looting...sorry."

"Fuck, Corporal Witherspoon, get your goddamned head out of your goddamned ass!"

"Yes, Sir."

"Tell Sergeant Hudson to form a perimeter, and tell Fourth Platoon to get their asses over there and help out."

"On it, Sir."

And the corporal went back to his radio as the captain went back to my forgery.

His brows wrinkled. "Do you mind if I call to confirm this order?"

I smiled. "Captain, I would expect you to. You'll find the number under the heading. But remember, it's an unsecured line. Do not mention the prisoner's name. We never know who may be listening."

He nodded and reached for a telephone receiver on the sergeant's desk. A few moments later, he put it back down on its cradle. "The number's busy."

I stifled my wicked grin. "Not surprising, Captain, everything going on. You got some coffee?"

He turned to one of the privates in the office area. "Private Ackles, get this man some coffee."

"Yes, Sir." The private shot out of his seat. "How does he take it?"

I answered, "Black, a little sugar."

I leaned against the sergeant's desk while the private brought me a steaming cup of joe. It was horrible, and confirmed, beyond reckoning, that this was an authentic US Army post. Ten minutes later the coffee cup was empty, and the captain still hadn't reached the general. Not surprising, since my old office's number had been out of service for over two years now.

"I'm sorry, Special Agent. The line's always busy."

I shook my head. "I wish I could say I'm surprised, Captain. The general was on the horn with Truman when I left."

"President Truman?"

Rolling my eyes, I snapped, "No, Jack Truman, the chief janitor. Who do you think? We got Russian troops surrounding Berlin, Captain. There's no way in or out, and war could kick off any time now."

Captain Padalecki lowered his head a bit. "Sorry, stupid question."

The kid by the radio piped up. "Captain, Sir, Fourth Platoon got lost on the way to the market, and now they got a Jeep with a flat tire."

"Fuck!" He spun away from me and faced the corporal. "Tell Sergeant Miller to just leave the goddamned Jeep for now. And if he can't read a goddamned map, tell him to hand it to some private who can, and then get his fucking platoon to the fucking market. How is First Platoon doing?"

The corporal spoke into the mike once more and then looked up. "Sir, Sergeant Hudson says they made three arrests, and the other looters backed off. He's got some German police assisting him now."

"Great," the captain shot back. "Ask Hudson if any of those kraut cops want Miller's job with Fourth Platoon. Because, so help me God, if that NCO fucks up one more time I'll give it to the first taker!"

Turning back to me, the captain asked, "What were we talking about?"

"You can't get through to General Clay's office," I said.

"Right, the goddamn phone is always busy with the president or something. Who knows?"

"Don't worry about it." I waved dismissively. "Listen, Captain, I'll be jake with you." I gestured for him to come closer and lowered my voice. "The general knows this Leer asshole is behind the whole thing."

He stepped back. "No shit?"

"No shit," I answered. "The sooner we get some answers from this Commie bastard, the sooner we can start solving these problems. Until then, the general is just trying to keep things calm. His boss has other ideas, you know. We have 'the bomb,' and Berlin might just be expendable."

"We would A-Bomb Berlin?" His jaw dropped. "I just don't see that happening."

I shrugged. "Better dead than Red."

Now, I just shut up and waited for him to reach the conclusions I wanted him to reach. This was a run of the mill army captain, who thought he might face World War III if he didn't make the right call. The captain picked up the phone and called the number one last time. He slammed it down but kept his fist on the receiver.

"I'm calling my battalion commander." He picked up the receiver and started dialing. My finger darted out to hang up the phone's cradle. His glare was a combination of rage and curiosity.

"Read those orders again, Captain. They say 'your eyes only.' Nobody is to know Mr. Leer or myself was ever here."

The corporal with the radio piped up. "Sir, I've got a message from Baker Company's CO—"

"Shut the fuck up, Witherspoon!"

The glare remained on me, but now the curiosity was gone. It had only rage. "Sergeant Jones!"

"Sir!" the sergeant responded.

"Get prisoner Leer out here. I want him handcuffed, and I want two privates to drive this special agent, and the prisoner, to General Clay's HQ in a Jeep." The sergeant just blinked at him. "Do it now, Jones!"

"Yes, Sir."

Two privates. Shit. The last thing I needed was company.

They brought Nigel out from the back of the stockade, his blond hair scruffy and his left eye blackened. His face only flashed a second of recognition when he saw me; then his eyes went back to the floor where they'd taken up residence.

The desk sergeant gave me some paperwork to sign, and I penned an illegible scrawl across the blank. Nobody had asked for my name, and I wasn't about to give it now. "Thanks, Sir," he said. "Private Ackles and Private Brewer will be accompanying you." He gestured toward two young men drawing M-3 submachine guns from the rack. "The Jeep will be in the motor pool."

"Thank you, Sergeant."

He turned to Nigel. "This guy is taking you across town. You give him any malarkey, and you'll have another shiner to match the one Padalecki gave you. Capisce?"

Nigel nodded, but his eyes never left the floor.

Private Brewer spoke up. "Excuse me, Sergeant. What do we do with his shit?"

"Huh?" The sergeant replied.

Brewer held up a small canvas bag. "The prisoner's personal items. Is he transferring to another facility or are we bringing him back here?"

Jones looked over his shoulder, but Captain Padalecki was already dealing with the next crisis and looking far too perturbed to be disturbed. He glanced at the canvas bag. "Just take it with you. If someone at HQ wants to sign for it, hand it over. If not, it comes back here."

Brewer nodded. "Okay, Sergeant."

The two privates stepped up to take control of the prisoner, and Sergeant Jones gave them a quick look over. "Ackles, close your dust cover."

Ackles checked his fly. "Huh?"

The sergeant rolled his eyes. "Your weapon's ejection-port cover, dip-shit. Also known as the M3's safety?"

"Oh, Sarge, I didn't even cock it." He stuck his finger in the ejection-port and flicked the bolt to the rear, then closed the cover. The M3 grease gun was the cheapest piece of garbage in the army's arsenal. Made of stamped metal parts, it looked more like a mechanic's tool than a soldier's weapon. It sprayed .45 caliber slugs in a generally forward direction, and you just hoped you'd hit something in the process. Still, it could kill you dead if just one bullet found its mark. It was .45 caliber, just like my pistol, and I had a fresh memory of what those bullets could do to somebody.

"Just keep it ready," Jones replied. "We don't know how crazy things are going to get out there. If you run into a bunch of rioting Germans or anything like that, turn the Jeep right around and come straight back. Okay?"

"Okay, Sergeant." Ackles nodded as he took hold of Nigel's arm. "We got this." Then turning to me, "You ready, Sir?"

"Yep." I was ready. Ready to shit a brick. How the hell was I supposed to get Nigel away from two GIs with sub-machine guns? I had to think fast.

We marched to the motor pool and climbed into a new Jeep with fresh paint and a canvas top. I sat in the front passenger seat while Ackles took the wheel. Brewer shoved Nigel in the back and joined him there.

Ackles pulled onto the road. Traffic was light to non-existent, as only army or police cars dared the roads. I guessed most Berliners had stocked up on essentials by now and were just hunkering down to see what joy the blockade brought next. Sweat poured down my face, but not from the afternoon's heat. We got about three blocks before I thought of a good idea. I just hoped it was good enough.

Snapping my fingers, I turned to our driver. "Private Ackles, you mind if we go back? I left my groceries in my car."

"Groceries, sir?"

"Yeah," I said. "I hit the PX this morning. As screwy as things are getting, I figured I better stock up on cigs and such while I could. It will just take a moment."

The soldier considered it and then shrugged. "Sure thing, sir."

He made a U-turn back to the barracks. Motoring around the block, I pointed out the black Volkswagen. The Jeep came to a stop right next to the old car, and I reassured Ackles. "Just take a sec."

He nodded and turned to look at the prisoner. Nigel sat next to Private Brewer, alert but not alarmed. I just hoped he was the pro I always took him for.

I took a few steps to the black car and leaned in through the window. Reaching for the grocery bag, I ripped it across the bottom then cradled it in my arms.

"Got it!" I announced.

Turning around, I took one step toward the Jeep before allowing the bag to fall apart in my grasp. "Shit!" I shouted as bread, peanut butter, cigarettes, and the two bottles of bourbon tumbled free. I tried to save the booze but was only half successful. One bottle shattered on the pavement, but the other came to rest on its base. As I bent to pick up the bread, I "accidentally" kicked the bottle so it rolled down the pavement, away from the Jeep.

"Goddamn it, Ackles, get that for me!"

He took the bait. The young MP got out and chased after the rolling bottle almost instinctively. Nigel let Private Ackles get a few steps and then rounded on Brewer with a violent twist. He spun on his captor like a tornado and, with both feet, kicked the private out of the Jeep and onto the pavement. Brewer tumbled into the street as I jumped into the driver's seat, stomped onto the clutch, and threw it in gear.

Just as Ackles grabbed my runaway liquor, he turned to see the Jeep speeding off and his buddy lying on the ground, moaning. I saw him in the rearview mirror as the bottle dropped with a smash and he went for the grease gun. Smaller and smaller the soldier shrank in my mirror. Ackles knelt, flipped up the dust cover, and aimed his weapon. With a roar, the M3 spat lead at our ass from half a block away.

I heard the slap of bullets smacking against the side of the Jeep but felt no pain, neither did I hear Nigel cry out, so I figured we were good. Catching a glimpse of Ackles changing magazines, I took the first left around the corner to get out of his sight.

Turning to me, Nigel said, "Good work, old man! Looks like you made a damn fine spy after all."

"Thanks."

"What's the plan from here, Shawn?"

"Beats the shit out of me, Mack. You get any bright ideas let me know."

Rounding another corner, I punched the gas. I wanted to get as much distance as possible between us and the McNair Barracks. Until something better came to mind, that was all the plan I had.

Nigel wasn't happy. "You mean, you haven't thought this through?"

"I got you out of jail."

"Out of the frying pan and into the fire, hmm." He shook his head. "Turn right up here."

I took his directions, another right, and then a few lefts. Soon we found ourselves on the southern edge of town. Trees became more plentiful and houses replaced apartment buildings as we left the capital city behind. "Okay, now we're in the suburbs.

"But how do you plan to get past the roadblocks?" I asked. "Berlin is still blockaded."

"This is an American Jeep."

"No shit Dick Tracy! And in other news, water is wet. So what?"

"Well, if I was you; I'd put it in four-wheel drive and take us off-road, old man. We can avoid the checkpoints and get well away from the city. From there, we're flying by the seat of our pants, I'm afraid."

"Nigel, old man, that's what I've been doing all this goddamned week!"

"Splendid; now who's Dick Tracy?"

I didn't answer him, just put it in "four-wheel high" and took us through someone's yard. That soon led to a clump of trees and a creek bed beyond. From there, I just tried to keep going in more or less a southern direction.

Now that I'd rescued the great spy, I began to reflect on my life's choices.

I could be in Paris right now. It was a beautiful summer day, and I might have tried my luck with some dame in a park. Or I could've just shoot the shit with Sands about baseball over a cup of coffee. But I wasn't in Paris. Hell, I wasn't even in France! I was in deep shit, and it was all this limey's fault. Or was it? To be honest, I didn't really know anymore, and that was driving me up the wall.

The creek bed was covered in little rocks, so the Jeep got some decent traction. Army Jeeps don't have doors, and our pants were under a constant naval assault from the water below. Nigel went rummaging in the glove compartment and found a paperclip attached to the Jeep's dispatch forms. It took him ten minutes to pick the locks on his handcuffs, but I bet it'd only have taken five if the Jeep wasn't bouncing around so much. We rumbled on for about half an hour, by which time my pants were ruined. I figured it likely we'd left the American Sector by then and were back in the Russian Zone—I hoped. Time to find a road or something.

As I took us out of the creek, the left rear tire gouged into the mud and got hung up like a politician in a brothel. The tire spun and spun, splattering mud everywhere and getting us nowhere. Of all the eloquent things I was capable of saying; I just screamed out a sincere, "Fuck!"

"Calm down, old man. Do we have a jack?"

"How the hell would I know? I just stole this car today!"

"Well, stop spinning the wheels and give me a chance to look."

My foot came off the gas as he got out of the Jeep and started poking around in the back. I sat in the driver's seat with my arms folded. Sure enough, the Jeep came equipped with all the usual army goodies: a crowbar, a pick, a shovel, and a jack. "Now, old man, get some stones for traction while I jack up the rear axle."

"Hey! I don't take orders from you, limey," I said while I climbed out of the vehicle and started collecting rocks. Good thing my feet were already soaked or the sensation of water seeping into my socks would have really pissed me off. Or was I already really pissed off?

Nigel stopped what he was doing. "I never said you should. What's the matter, Shawn?"

"Nothing! Not a goddamned thing! I'm about to be declared a deserter. I just committed treason to get you out of the hoosegow. And now we're stuck in this godforsaken forest with a stolen Jeep that won't fucking move! Oh, I'm just dandy." I dropped the rocks at his feet and they landed with a splash that reached to our shirts.

He took a step back. "I'm grateful, old man, but I didn't ask you to spring me. In fact, I didn't ask for you to get caught up in any of this mess at all! So, why did you do it?"

"Because I believed you, Nigel! Because I'm trying to do a good job. Because I lied to the first woman I ever slept with. And because I fucking killed two men yesterday morning!"

We stood there, feet in the cold creek, while I regained a little of my composure.

"I am sorry, Shawn. This isn't how I planned things either."
I nodded.

Nigel went back to jacking up the Jeep. Then, he picked up the rocks I'd gathered and wedged them under the tires. He lowered the Jeep and put the jack back where it had come from. "Give it a try now, won't you, Shawn?"

Silently, I nodded. I guess I'd said all I had to say. All I could say.

We got back in the Jeep, and I drove it up the bank. The closest thing to a street was a narrow path that wound around the wilderness. I followed it, hoping it went somewhere useful. When we emerged from the bushes, there was a farm surrounded by wheat fields, sitting pretty about a mile away. I stopped the Jeep, and we looked each other in the eye.

He took a deep breath. "I have a week and two days before my NKVD handler expects me in Warsaw. That's just enough time to warn my network, I hope. Naturally, the meet I planned from London is down the tubes now. I'll have to contact them each directly. What about you? What are you going to do now, Shawn?"

Good question. Long-term, I hadn't the foggiest idea. Short term, that was easier. Looking down at my muddy, wrinkled, oversized, sweat-stained blue suit made me want to cry. I felt disgusting. "Do you have any money?"

Nigel reached into the back seat for the canvas bag that held his personal property. Removing his wallet, he opened it to reveal a wad of dough in currencies I hadn't seen before. He rubbed his black eye. "Your military police might be a bit brutish, but they aren't thieves. We should be set for quite a while."

I nodded. "Good. Let's go find a room or something and get clean."

CHAPTER NINE

"Do you speak any German?"

"Nine."

"Oh God." Nigel's head went into his hand. "You can't even say 'no' in German without that terrible American accent. Where are you from again?"

"Boston."

"I'm glad your president doesn't sound anything like that. I don't think there's a man from England to Australia who could understand a word he spoke, and it just might start a war, what."

I shrugged.

"Very well." His eyes turned to the farmhouse. "Let's hide the Jeep, and take a stroll down this country lane. When we get to the farmhouse, don't say anything."

"Won't that seem a little odd?" I asked. "Folks would at least expect me to say hello."

"Best not to risk it." He paused in thought until an idea struck him. "I'll tell them we served together in Stalingrad, and you haven't spoken since. Shellshock and all, hmm?"

I blinked. "Impersonating German war veterans?"

"It works for cover. We're of the right age, probably former SS or something, but I shouldn't need to go into that. Best to keep things vague and let their imaginations do the work for us. And it will explain why we're on the run."

My jaw dropped. "Why the hell are you going to tell them we're on the run?"

Nigel heaved a great sigh. "Shawn, look at us. We're muddy, tired, and hungry. Of course we're on the run. The question is from who and why. If I tell them the Allies are hunting us, good German folk will be inclined to give us shelter. Most of them have mixed feelings about the Nazis…at best. But it's a natural inclination to favor one's countrymen over foreign occupiers."

I mulled it over. "Makes sense."

"Good. Now I'm going to tell them your name is Hans, so be sure to look at whoever calls you by that name. You're playing a mute, not a deaf. Oh, and just remember to raise your hand, like so, whenever someone says 'Heil Hitler.'" He gave a discreet Nazi salute and my stomach went queasy.

We ditched the Jeep in a depression just off the trail. I suggested we cover it with branches, but Nigel figured it would be too much bother, and that we'd be long gone by the time it was discovered. From there, it was a short walk to the old red brick and Tudor farmhouse.

This place was in every way opposite of the farmhouse outside of Stieglitz. It was a well-maintained property with a two story house and a sturdy barn. I didn't see any tractors, but they had some horses stabled that looked like they could handle a plow or whatever. As we came round the bend, a kid about five years old, in lederhosen, saw us and ran inside the house. A moment later a man stood in the doorway with a big hammer in his hand. I hoped he'd been doing home repairs when we showed up...but I knew he probably wasn't.

The farmer was a good six feet tall and stout, with a big mustache. He shouted a challenge that Nigel answered in perfect Kraut-talk. I couldn't follow much, but the big German's tone went from harsh to mellow, to welcoming as Nigel worked his magic spell of English blarney. I just nodded whenever Nigel pointed to me and looked up whenever I heard "Hans." Nobody did the "Heil Hitler" shtick and I was glad of that.

The farmer led us inside, and I've got to say I was impressed. Polished, hardwood floors rose to meet my feet. The whole place was spotless and well decorated in that German folk style. I swear, there was even one of those cuckoo clocks on the wall. It was half past seven in the evening—the tail end of another very long day.

More babbling in German and the housewife brought us some clean towels. She was a pretty thing, maybe thirty years old with an ample bosom, yet she wore a stiff, wooden smile. Nigel clicked his heels and gave her a small bow, and I followed his lead. Well, I bowed anyway; I didn't have any idea how to get that "snap" to come out of my shoes. Two young men entered the room and just stared at us. One was a teenager who might have been lucky enough to miss the war. His older brother, however, had probably served in Hitler's army...he was missing a leg.

The father barked some orders and the teenager grabbed two buckets and went outside. Nigel turned to me, spoke some German that I pretended to understand, then gestured us toward the stairs. We went to the second floor and found the bathroom. There was a tub with an old-fashioned pump, some soap, and more towels. I went to work the lever, but nothing came of it. Then, I looked out the window to see the teenager pouring water to prime it.

Nigel whispered to me. "You go first. I'll wait in the hall and answer their questions. By the time you're done, they should be satisfied to leave you alone while you wait for me."

The water was cold, but oh, so welcome. I hadn't had a full-fledged bath since I left my hotel room in Frankfort, and to just finally get clean felt amazing. Outside, I could hear Nigel lying to the housewife in German as I reintroduced my nethers to a thing called soap. Toweling off, I heard a knock. I opened it a crack to see Nigel handing me some clean workman's clothes and an old cap. Not even risking a "*danke*," I just smiled and nodded. A few minutes later, I swapped places with Nigel.

I squatted against the wall and let my face fall into my palms. Jesus H. Christ, what a day it'd been. Hell, a week, almost a month now. How long ago did I get hit by a little gray car in Rethel? When did I lose my virginity...a day, a week after that? By now I'd gone so far down the rabbit-hole that the Mad Hatter looked sane. To add to the fun, I was lost behind enemy lines while a fugitive British secret agent took a bath not three yards from me. Could anything else possibly go wrong in my life?

Looking up, I saw a pair of innocent blue five-year-old eyes fixed upon mine. The kid held a toy bear in one hand and was playing with his lip with the other. Maybe he was four, I don't know, but he wasn't scared of the big stranger who sat by the bathroom door wearing his daddy's old dungarees. I smiled.

Just then, his mother arrived to lead the tot away by the hand. As she marched him down the stairs, the little boy looked over his pudgy little shoulder and smiled right back at me. My God, maybe there was some hope left in this shitty little world after all.

***

Nigel emerged, looking the image of a rustic German peasant. Hell, he seemed born to play the role as he chatted up the family and got us invited to dinner. The food was all that good, wholesome stuff that can only be found on a farm; fresh barley bread, green salad, roast ham, and a glass of cool milk to wash it all down. Nigel took the lead in dinner conversation, regaling them with what must have been really funny stories that had 'em rolling. I played along as best I could, keying on the tone of what people said, not the words. Nobody asked me to speak. It seemed Nigel had done a good job of selling the "traumatized war veteran" thing. Occasionally, I caught a glance of pity, but never from the guy with the missing leg.

We were given the children's room to bed down for the night. There was only one small bed, but the family was nice enough to set up a cot next to it. Nigel took that cot and offered me the bed, maybe because he felt he still owed me for busting him out of jail—if so, he had an excellent point.

"So far, so good, hmm?"

I whispered back, "Yeah, but tell me where you learned German so good?"

"From my mother, old man. She was a war-bride. My father met her when Her Majesty's forces took the Kaiser's colony in South West Africa back in '17. She was born in Germany but lived most of her life abroad. From her, I got my German and French. But I'll tell you, Shawn, it was hell learning Czech."

"When did you learn that?"

"During the war. By '44 I was out of the regular army per-se and with Military Intelligence exclusively, working with the partisans. Didn't speak a word of the language at first. Had to pick it up on the go, hmm. Devilishly tricky grammar. What do you speak?"

"Just English, some high school French, and a few smithereens of Gaelic."

He frowned. "Not too likely to run into any Celts where I'm going, I'm afraid."

"And where is that?" I asked.

He gave me a long look. "You already know most of my story. I'm heading east to warn my network before the secret police sweep them up. Rather not tell you any more until I know your story a little better though."

"What's to tell? I'm like Geronimo, an Indian that's gone off the reservation. I had orders to follow you up until I got to Rethel, back in France. After that, I was told to just leave well enough alone and come back to base. I exceeded my orders, and you know the rest."

"If you go back, they're likely to throw you in the slammer. You know that, Shawn?"

I nodded and took a long breath. "Yep."

He seemed to consider that for a moment. "I don't see how you can get in any worse trouble at this point in the game...."

"Thanks."

"...so an extra week wouldn't make much difference. I could use someone watching my back for the next few days; it's going to be a little tricky, old man. But if we're lucky, we may even find some information that has enough value to mitigate your situation somewhat. Better when the Prodigal Son returns with a gift for his master than otherwise, hmm?"

"I think you're confusing the Prodigal Son with the parable about the talents."

He raised an eyebrow. "You know your Bible?"

"Altar boy, St. Catharine's parish. Until Ronny Kelley stole the communion wine and I got the rap for it."

"My, my, you are full of surprises." He stretched out on the cot and fluffed his pillow. "So, are you up for the game? Or shall we part company in the morning?"

As I pulled my blanket up and stared at the ceiling, I thought about that. Nigel had a good point. There wasn't any way I was going to become a hero in the eyes of the army, but if I could bring back some valuable intelligence, I might not be a complete goat either. Salvation like that wouldn't get me into army heaven, but I might only have to go to purgatory for a while, instead of army hell.

"I'm with you, Nigel. Now, where are we going?"

"Prague."

***

Come the next morning the one-legged son was at the reins of the family's hay wagon. Nigel and I sat in the back, while the pretty wife handed us each a breakfast of biscuits and sausage wrapped in a napkin. She still wore that same wooden grin, as if she remembered how people smiled but, somehow over the years, she'd forgotten why. Nigel thanked her profusely, while I showed my mute appreciation as best I could. The youth cracked the whip and we headed down the dusty road and over a hill.

Just as we crested that hill, an army Jeep, with a red Russian star instead of the American's white, arrived at the big farmhouse. Two Russian officers got out. The youth noticed the Russians too. He spat a vicious curse but kept the wagon moving.

Nigel asked him what was going on, and he and the youth proceeded to have a highly animated Teutonic conversation. It ended with Nigel and the youth glaring at the Soviet car with impotent rage. I later found out the reason this family's farm had been spared the typical Soviet degradations. The local Red Army commander had taken a shine to the farmer's wife.

Her infidelity guaranteed her family's safety, and nothing else would.

***

We arrived at a small town train station, and Nigel bought us tickets to Prague. This time I didn't fear losing the sneaky Brit on the train. We sat side by side for the next seven hours. To be honest, it was the most relaxed seven hours I'd spent since the start of this fiasco. Nigel brought us some sandwiches and cigarettes from the dining car while we enjoyed watching the countryside go by. The further we got from Berlin the better our view became. Czechoslovakia hadn't been raped by the Ruskies like Germany had. In fact, I noticed a lot of German POWs, still in their old Wehrmacht uniforms, working the fields on behalf of their new masters. Too bad for them.

Then came Prague.

We rolled out of the hills and looked down to see a great city in the valley below. There were several large bridges crossing a wide river, and our train was heading for one of 'em. I was amazed to see so many of the buildings in such good shape. In fact, I only saw one totally destroyed from old bomb damage. Not even Paris looked this good from a distance, and I wondered who the people of Prague had paid off to keep the armies of Europe away these past few years.

When we arrived at the central train station, I felt like a hick from Hoboken as I gawked around the place. The station looked more like a cathedral than a lot of churches I'd knelt in. Statues of saints looked down on the weary travelers with compassionate eyes while the crowd muddled below. I almost felt sacrilegious in my old farmer's clothes and cheap cap.

A few Russian flatfoots hung around, but nobody asked to see our passports. In fact, the cops were too busy making time with the dames to notice much at all—least wise, two western spies walking right under their noses.

Nigel did all the talking, He picked up a trolley schedule. It was obvious he'd been here before, but he still got a map and handed it to me while he took a few moments to study the schedule. I gave the map a quick once-over. This was a big town, and a fellow could get lost. Pulling me aside, he said, "We have to make a stop in the old town square, then I suggest a comfortable hotel and room service."

I smiled. "No argument from me, buddy."

We took the trolley into town and soon found ourselves in this gorgeous old city square. I swear Quincy Market had nothing on this place. Beautiful old buildings like something out of a *Three Musketeers* movie surrounded us. There was even a grand old cathedral with towers looming over the stately, yellow-bricked hotels. Nigel led me to a spot on the pavement where twenty-seven white crosses were fixed into the cobblestones. He knelt down like he was praying, then took out a piece of chalk from his pocket. Circling a cross, he gave me a wink. Then we walked off to find a hotel.

Nigel didn't skimp. He set us up in a nice place just off the old town square and got us a room on the second floor. It was clear the hotel clerk had a little trouble following his Czech, but his money spent as well as anybody's and we were soon locking the room's door behind us. I collapsed into a well-upholstered desk chair next to the second bed.

"Nigel, this ain't bad."

He didn't relax but went about the room in a brusque manner, inspecting the windows, the bathroom, and the telephone in that order. Over his shoulder, he said, "Glad you like it, old man."

"What are you doing?"

His task done, he sat on the edge of the bed and lit a cigarette. "Checking the room. What did it look like?"

"For what?"

He looked at me as if I were a retarded child. "The windows, to ensure they would open, the bathroom to see if the adjoining room has access, and the telephone to see if it's bugged or is otherwise a party line. Where did you learn your tradecraft?"

I shrugged. "Fort Devens, Massachusetts. They mostly taught us how to interview people and write reports."

Nigel shook his head as he took a long drag on the cloven scented, European smoke. I lit one out of sympathy. They weren't Lucky Strikes, but a smoke is a smoke when you need one.

"That's a good start, Shawn. But it's hardly the whole game. Do you know why I drew that circle around the cross?"

"Nope," I replied. "Don't even know what those crosses were for. But I'm listening."

"Oh, the crosses commemorate some local heroes, beheaded hundreds of years ago if I recall. My agent passes by that way every day. If he sees a circle around the third cross, he knows to meet me at a certain tavern at ten o'clock on the following evening. He's a balding man about fifty years old with a gray mustache and thick, black-framed glasses. His suits are always either dark blue or black, and he's fond of outlandish bowties in purples, oranges, and such. He'll be carrying a newspaper in his right hand, and he will be alone. At least, that's my hope."

"Okay, where do I fit in?"

"You, my American friend, are going to sit on a bench, that I'll show you, at a trolley stop from nine thirty until midnight. Unless something happens sooner. From there, you'll have a good view of my agent as he approaches. If he's not alone, or if he is not carrying a newspaper in his right hand, you will light a cigarette. I will be in a position to see you, but not him. If you light that cigarette, the meet is off, and you and I will scatter to meet back at the twenty-seven crosses in Old Town Square at two in the morning, and no sooner."

"You think he'll be followed or something?"

"I have no idea, Shawn. It's just my way of being careful. And in this business, your choices are to either be careful or be dead."

Sounded like good advice to me, but another thought occurred to me. "What if I see some cops, or whoever, show up after you start to talk to the guy?"

"If you see anybody paying undue attention to our meet, casually walk into the tavern and use the bathroom. I'll be in a position to watch you enter as I'm talking to him. If I see you in the tavern, I'll make my excuses and leave as quickly as I can. In such a case, we will also meet back at the crosses at two in the morning."

"Why so late?"

"Because, old man, if you or I are being followed, that should be enough time to shake a tail. If one of us should fail to rendezvous, the other will assume an arrest has taken place and will act accordingly. In your case, if I don't return, I'd recommend you get back to Berlin's American Sector as best you can. If I do not see you, I will assume you've been compromised and you will never see me again. Now, shall we order room service?"

The food was pretty good, some kind of roast beef and a soup with a lot of beets in it. We also had a bottle of fine cognac, labeled 1922. Nigel and I talked a bit, smoked some cigs, and downed the booze. He wasn't a bad fellow really, once you got to know him, except he lacked any understanding of baseball, and thought "A Lovely Bunch of Coconuts" counted as a pretty good song. I tried to set him straight, of course, but he'd have none of it.

"What? And your people with those silly tin whistles going 'tootly-toot' qualifies as Irish musical culture, Shawn? I think not!"

"First of all, you filthy-crumpet-stuffer, when I was talking about my people, I meant Americans, and only the really handsome ones are Irish! Now, do you honestly think any of that 'jolly, jolly sixpence' crap can compare with great tunes like 'Sing Sing Sing' by Benny Goodman, or Cab Calloway's 'Minnie the Moocher'?"

"'Minnie the Moocher'? Oh, my Lord! You're asked to put up an example of 'your people's' musical inheritance, and the best you can do is, 'hidy-hidy-hidy-ho'?"

I leaned back and took a long drag on my cig. "You'll see, Nigel, me boy. You'll see. Our music's gonna' crash onto your shores like a harmonic D-Day, and blow the bobby socks off every kid in London town."

He folded his arms. "Well, we'll see if we can't counter that."

***

When I opened my eyes the next morning, the first thing I saw was the empty cognac bottle. I wished it was an aspirin bottle, but no such luck. Despite my Irish heritage, I never could drink more than a few shots of hard liquor without getting a hangover, and that Czech stuff was killer. Nigel still slept in his bed, blond hair covering his eyes as the sun shone through the window. Fine by me; that gave me first dibs on the shower.

When I came out, Nigel caught a glimpse of me in nothing but a towel with soap dripping down my ear. "Good morning, sunshine. And how are we this morning, hmm?"

"We are hung over, and there ain't no aspirin in the bathroom. But I think we'll live. How 'bout you?"

"Fair to middling, Shawn. It takes more than half a bottle of cognac to bowl me down."

I rubbed my head. "Well, my mother broke family tradition and raised me on milk. So what's the plan for today?"

"Not much until the meet. We need to check out of here and find another hotel. Also, we should buy some local clothes to blend in with the populace a little better. Then case the tavern so that I can be assured nothing has changed since I was last there, and read the local papers to see if there's any news of arrests for espionage."

"Can we at least get some grub first?"

He raised an eyebrow at me.

Damn, I swore sometimes it was like Nigel didn't speak English at all. "Breakfast, Nigel, can we get some breakfast?"

"Of course, old man. I'll order room service. It's always better than risking exposure in the hotel restaurant."

He made the call, then jumped in the shower himself. By the time he'd toweled off the tray had arrived, and we enjoyed some funny little jam filled biscuits and poached eggs with coffee. Nigel made me check the room to make sure we left nothing behind. He was especially concerned about my badge and passport. "I'd rather they found your gun, old man. All that would tell them is that some bloody cowboy had slept here last night."

Holstering the pistol, I said, "Sorry, old man, but I'm signed for this rod. It's an Article Fifteen offense if I lose it."

"A what?"

I thought about it but decided to skip the full explanation. "In your army, it'd probably be a flogging."

Rolling his eyes, Nigel opened the door, and we said goodbye for good to our first Prague hotel room.

Next, we went shopping. I played the mute once again as Nigel picked out some nice, but not too nice, suits of local cut. He whispered that the idea was to dress like just over half of the people around us did. That seemed like a good idea to me. It took forever to get everything we needed; suitcases, clothes, shoes, cigarettes. Everything was in different shops. Apparently, the Czechs had never heard of a department store.

We ate lunch at an open-air café. It was loud and busy, so anybody listening would have to strain to hear us. Nigel whispered to me as he read the paper, "Looks like the Reds still have a stranglehold on Berlin. The RAF and the American Air Corps are flying in supplies, but the Russians don't take that as any kind of threat. Stalin predicts the West will capitulate by the end of the month."

"Air Force."

He looked up from the paper. "I beg your pardon?"

"As of last year, it's the US Air Force. New service; they're not part of the US Army anymore. We did this whole reorganization after the war; new departments, new intelligence agencies, the works. So, what are the Allies doing besides flying in a few planes?"

His eyes went back to the paper. "Not much. There's a rumor about an American Army unit prepared to invade the Russian Zone to liberate Berlin, but Stalin threatens war if they dare try."

"And we have the bomb."

He frowned. "Yes, there is that."

We didn't discuss it any further. What more was there to say? That World War III could break out at any moment was scary, and if it did, we were on the wrong side of the bombing range. But what the hell were we supposed to do about it? The good news was that the local press didn't report on any arrests of western spies. If they were rolling up Nigel's network, they were taking their sweet time about it.

"If I were the NKVD station chief, old man, I'd put the western agents under surveillance for a few weeks before making arrests. That way, I could find out who else was involved before swooping in. When the arrests did come, I'd do it all in one night, before the agents could warn each other. Then, I'd make sure it made the headlines—as a warning to others who would spy for the West, and as a way to advance my own career in the party."

I thought about that. "Makes sense. So you're acting under the assumption that your guy is gonna' be tailed tonight."

"Tonight and every night. The information was leaked over a month ago. I'm sure it's filtered through the Bolshevik bureaucracy by now."

"What do you know about this MI5 traitor, Nigel?"

"No names in public, old man." He shook his head. "Not much. I received an anonymous phone call last spring, from someone trying to recruit me to their side. It seemed he knew of certain…habits of mine and was attempting to blackmail me. I kept him talking for as long as I could, and this anonymous person revealed that he already knew the names of my agents in the East.

When he realized I was getting more information from him that he meant to share, he hung up before I could accept or decline his offer."

"Not much to go on," I said.

"No, it's not."

"And did Mr. Anonymous pull the trigger on that blackmail?" I wanted to know.

Nigel looked me square in the eye. "He didn't, but secrets don't always keep regardless. I paid a price. But I will not betray my country; not then, not now, not ever." And there was steel in every word he said.

***

The location for the meet was Nigel in a nutshell, very discreet.

The tavern was in the basement of a building that might have been older than the US Constitution. Access to its front door came from an alleyway, and only a small sign announced the entrance at all. Inside, I saw a stone-worked cavern with a low ceiling and rows of wooden tables illuminated with flickering candles sticking out of old wine bottles. The crowd was mostly old men killing time smoking long pipes, drinking beer, and playing chess. To me, it was like stepping into the middle ages, and I half expected Friar Tuck to come up, shake my hand, and offer me a turkey leg.

Nigel ordered a couple of beers, and we sat down near the back of the place where it was darkest. I noticed a door just over Nigel's shoulder and a sooty fireplace to my right, but nothing remarkable about the place in general. As we quietly sipped our brews, a waitress opened the door, letting sunshine dance on Nigel's back as she headed up the stairs carrying a tray. When the beer was done, Nigel got up and headed across the room while I followed. He took a left turn down a short hallway that led to the restroom. We used the facilities while an old cat hissed at us from behind the window's blue curtains.

When we left the tavern, Nigel quizzed me like a school teacher.

"How many exits did you count?"

I blinked in the bright sun. After the dim light of the tavern, my eyes needed to adjust. "Uh, two...I think."

He shook his head. "Four, old man; the customer entrance, the service door, and the bathroom window.

"That's only three."

Nigel looked past me toward the building we'd just left. "The women's bathroom is in line with the men's. Look over your shoulder. Do you see how the basement windows are placed on this building?"

I turned to see the outside of the blue curtained windows. There were two sets of them. "Oh, thanks, I didn't notice."

"How many employees in the tavern?"

I thought about it. I saw a bartender and two waitresses, but that was all. "Three?"

"Very good. Did any of them look like a bouncer or what not?"

The waitresses, no, but the bartender looked like he was in pretty good shape. "Maybe the bartender in a pinch, but no bouncers exactly."

"Correct. Now the patrons; did any of them look like police detectives or perhaps gangsters? Believe me, either would be trouble."

As a city kid, I knew the look of guys like that. Men in their twenties to thirties dressed slightly better than anyone around them, who had the confidence of guys totally in charge of their situation. "No."

"Smashing. Now, let me show you to your post."

He led me to a bench at the trolley stop and pointed out where I should expect his agent to approach from. I got the idea that Nigel would be waiting in the alley, but he wasn't too specific about that.

The day's work done, we found another hotel and got another room on the second floor. Nigel ordered room service but this time we passed on the cognac. We drank coffee instead as we waited for evening to descend over Prague.

***

Sitting at the trolley stop with a newspaper in my hands, I watched the stars come out while pretending I could read Czech by a streetlight. Nigel and I had parted company over an hour ago. He insisted we take alternate routes to the meet, and that seemed like a good idea to me. Checking my watch only made me nervous, but I did it anyway. It was eight minutes after ten, and no sign of Nigel's agent. Reaching into my pocket, I took my last cigarette from the pack. I was just about to light it when I remembered that would scrub the meet. Shit, I really could use a smoke too.

Then, I saw him; dark suit, gray mustache, thick glasses, bright pink bowtie, and a newspaper in his right hand. And, thank God, he was alone. I put my cigarette in its pack and went back to pretending to read the paper. Out of the corner of my eye, I saw the guy turn into the alley that led to the tavern. So far so good.

A trolley stopped by and a bunch of folks got out. One guy sat on the bench beside me and tried to chat me up. I would've obliged if I'd understood a damn word he said. After a while, he gave up and began reading a book. When the next trolley came, he bugged out and good riddance.

Checking my watch again, I discovered that Nigel and company had spent at least a half hour together. I was just wondering how much longer this was going to take when the cops arrived. I could hardly miss 'em…two bruisers in their mid-thirties in double-breasted suits and nice fedoras. They had that cocky air of men who were used to pushing people around, and their eyes kept scanning the area like lions looking for a gazelle. They paused outside the alley and one pointed toward the tavern door. This was not good.

Getting up, I carefully folded my paper and tucked it under my arm, right next to where my gun rested in its holster. I turned toward the alley and made a beeline for the tavern at a nice, relaxed pace. Entering the smoky room, I did a quick glance around for Nigel. He sat at the same table we'd shared that afternoon, drinking beer with his new pink bow-tied buddy. I wasn't jealous. I went to the john. When I came out, Nigel and Mr. Bowtie were gone, and the two detectives were interrogating the bartender.

Time for me to go.

I strolled right out of the place and just kept walking. The narrow streets of Prague twisted and turned in crazy ways, sometimes taking the form of staircases instead of sidewalks. I took no chances. Having been the follower, I had a pretty good idea of what to do on the other side of the equation. I did everything I could think of to frustrate anyone who might be shadowing me, but I never spotted a tail.

After a while, my route looked like a plate of spaghetti dumped onto a map, and I was thoroughly lost myself. Fortunately, I still had the map Nigel had given me. A little land navigation and I was back at the old town square with over an hour to spare. It was twelve fifty-one in the morning, and Nigel wouldn't be there 'til two.

Looking around, I saw no one else was hanging around in the square. If I stayed out in the open, I might just draw attention I didn't want. I needed to find a place of sanctuary to hole up until two, a place where I could be discreet. I looked around and saw that place looming over my shoulder.

St. Nicholas' Cathedral was huge, as big as Fenway Park and much more beautiful. Walking into the chapel, I was greeted by bone-white stone walls with gold overlays that towered up a good four stories. The ceiling was expertly painted with images of heaven itself, and hundreds of candles filled the air with the musky odor of beeswax. This joint had St. Catherine's beat, hands down.

Still, if you know the layout of one Catholic church you know 'em all.

The confessionals were to the left.

I stepped into a booth and crossed myself out of habit. For a moment, I just sat there, wondering what my next move would be. I checked my watch again; just under an hour now. Taking a deep breath, I leaned my head against the polished wood of the booth, closed my eyes, and let out a long, tired breath. This would do for a hiding place; yes sir, this would do.

Then the priest spoke up.

Shit! I meant damn...no! I meant...nuts. I didn't expect a priest to be on duty at that time of night. Through the confessional screen, I heard his scratchy old voice, asking me for my confession—in perfect Czechoslovakian. Not understanding a word of what he said didn't mean I didn't catch his drift. He was insistent, and you don't say no to a priest, not when you're in God's house. Besides, I had a lot to unload.

"Forgive me, Father, for I have sinned."

Through the screen, I plainly heard him say, "Huh?"

"It's been...oh, I don't know, maybe eight months since my last confession."

He babbled something else in Czech.

"Frankly, Father, I'm glad you don't speak English. Oh, don't get me wrong. I'm sure you respect the sanctity of the confessional and all. But you see, Father, a lot of what I'm about to say is classified, and it's just better this way."

"*Sprechen sie Deutsch?*"

"No, Father. I don't speak German either. Anyway, I'm a soldier who's AWOL from the army; which isn't as bad as desertion, but almost. You see, I was on this mission to catch a Commie spy, except it turned out he's not a Commie spy. That part's a long story, I guess. Anyway...." I took a moment to collect my thoughts, "I've had sinful fornication with a woman. I suppose part of my sin is that I don't really feel bad about that, but I do feel bad that I lied to her, and that I used her. You see, she really was a Commie spy, and I needed information. True, she set me up by putting a dead body in the car's trunk and not telling me about it, but I didn't know she'd do that at the time, so the sin is still on me, you see?"

I think the next language the priest tried was Polish, but that didn't get him anywhere either.

"But that's not the worst of it, Father. I killed a man. Well, I killed two men, but the first one doesn't bother me so much because that was self-defense; he came at me with a knife. The second guy I rubbed out. Well...Father, that one bugs me a lot. You see, he wasn't trying to kill me. Well, he might have killed me if he'd had the chance, but he never had the chance. I just popped him right in the back of the head when he came in the door. I mean, what kind of guy does that?"

This time the priest went back to Czech, but his hopes of understanding me were obviously as dead as Lazarus, but without hope of resurrection.

"I know, Father. God doesn't like killing. But He approves if it's in a good cause, right? I mean, that's what the Crusades were all about, a good cause? And I know fornication is bad too. I'm not sure I can say that was for a good cause because I was pretty horny. Sorry, Father, I don't mean to be crude. I mean to say, I was really tempted. That's no excuse, I know, but there it is.

"Anyway, Father, I'm real sorry, and I'm not just saying that, Father. I am. I wish I'd never gotten into this mess. It all started because I was just trying to do a good job. You understand that, don't you, Father?"

There was a long pause before the priest replied with something else I couldn't understand. Maybe it was Czech for "Just get on with it, pal."

"Okay, Father, I know it's kind of hard to give me penance when you can't understand a word I'm saying. But God understands. Don't he? I mean, he understands that I'm trying to make things right? If I can just get Nigel safely on his way that will make up for it, right? Then I'll go back to the army and take my licking. That should be penance enough in the eyes of God, right?"

This time the priest spoke Latin, and I'd heard the phrase before. *"Vade et amplius iam noli peccare."* I bowed my head and prayed for the Lord's forgiveness, and I went out, hoping to sin no more.

"Amen."

CHAPTER TEN

"Another five minutes and our partnership would've been over, old man."

I checked my watch. "It's two on the nose."

"Exactly." With a tilt of his head, he set us in the direction of the Old Town Hall and its much-lauded astrological clock tower. We kept walking, block after block in a twisting, turning route. Every now and then Nigel stopped to look in a store window. He never seemed as interested in the merchandise, but he was fascinated by the reflections in the glass. While ostensibly peering at a display of women's underwear, he said, "I only spotted two in the tavern, did you see anymore?"

"No, just those two guys in double-breasted suits. Can't say for sure they were even looking for us, but I figured it best not to take chances."

He nodded. "You have good instincts. I'll give you that. My agent had time to get his warning, and I even managed to receive some fair intelligence from him before we parted."

My eyebrow shot up. "Anything of interest?"

"That depends on how fascinated you are by Czechoslovakian political maneuverings. Since President Benis was forced out last winter, the Communists have been flexing their muscles quite a lot. My agent seems to think that President Gottwald plans a series of purges; first to remove non-Communists, then some prominent Communists like old Rudolf Slánský, who is somewhat less pliable to Moscow." He shook his head. "Things are growing very cold in this world, Shawn. I can't say how all this will end, but I imagine it will be quite a long time before things even begin to thaw out."

I shrugged. "The Commies have been hard at work; I'll give 'em that. But I can't see why they're kicking so much dirt in our faces. Weren't we just the best of buddies two or three years ago?"

Nigel let out a short chuckle. "Wars make strange bedfellows, old man. Not long ago I was training Communist guerrillas to fight the Nazis."

"I know; remember, Romana and I talked?"

"Yes, you did mention her, hmm. I met her during the war at one of our training camps in England. When the NKVD took me on as a defector last month, she was the one they sent to sneak me out of Great Britain. They thought that since I knew her, I'd be more likely to trust her." He turned to his left and we kept walking through the twisting moonlit streets.

"Do you?"

He blinked. "Do I what, old man?"

"Do you trust Romana?"

"Ha! Only as far as I can throw her. She is quite the hardcore Communist. It's the very air she breathes, you see? I'm sure she thinks herself quite noble, all that 'sacrifice for the good of the people' nonsense. In her mind, every capitalist is as bad as the Nazis that killed her parents, and every Bolshevik is struggling for the common good of all mankind. A very black and white outlook on a very gray situation. She's braver than she is smart but quite ruthless. How you managed to get any information out of her is a mystery to me."

My eyes went to my shoes, but I didn't answer him. I'd done enough confessing for one night.

***

It was past four in the morning when we finally got back to the hotel room. I flopped onto the bed, but Nigel went straight to the phone. What followed was a quick Czech conversation wherein Nigel seemed to have dialed the wrong number or something before quickly hanging up. Turning to me he said, "We're done here. Get your things and let's go."

"What's the problem, Nigel?"

"The problem is, if anyone manages to trace that call back to this room we'd best be elsewhere."

"Who did you call?"

He grabbed his suitcase. "I'll tell you later. Right now, just go."

I didn't have much in the way of possessions. The few outfits Nigel bought for me yesterday fit neatly into the suitcase he'd also provided. We were checked out and on the move within ten minutes.

Once safely on the street, he confided, "I just called my next agent and told him I need to give him some information. We'll pass him on the Charles Bridge tomorrow morning at eight. Right now, let's just get some sustenance and find a new room."

By this point, I was tired, hungry, and generally feeling like I'd been beaten with a stick. Nigel must've been feeling it too. He took us to an all-night joint with a balcony that overlooked the town. We got some eggs and coffee. The food was good, but the coffee was great, giving me the chance to feel halfway human again. I thought I could give up cigarettes any time, but not coffee—not ever. We didn't talk for fear of someone picking up my American accent. Sitting in silence as the sun rose over the old, majestic city, we watched storm clouds rolling in. But just then, it only made our sunrise all the more spectacular, with beautiful pinks and oranges smeared across a golden sky. The medieval towers of Prague silhouetted against the sunlight, and for a moment, I really did feel like I'd been transported back in time to some fairytale land of make-believe. When every day of freedom might be your last, you cherish the little things.

I sipped another cup of Bohemian coffee in silence, and Nigel smoked one of his fancy rolled cigarettes while we took in the view.

After the check was paid, but before my stomach could completely settle, Nigel guided me down the streets of Prague to another hotel. We found a nice one near the river. But when Nigel discovered that their second floor was all booked up, we left. Finally, we settled for a rundown place near a meat packing plant on the south end of town. The wallpaper smelled of mold, but it had a second story room.

As I threw my suitcase on the bed, I asked, "What is it with you and second-floor hotel rooms?"

"Tradecraft," he said. "The first floor is vulnerable to intrusion from the outside. The third floor is hard to escape from, and you can be easily trapped. But you can always jump out of a second story window in a pinch. Never know when you'll be betrayed and have to make a run for it, old man."

"Well, thanks, Nigel," I replied as I kicked off my shoes. "That will sure help me sleep at night."

He smiled. "Shawn, my good man, if you're not paranoid by nature, this isn't the job for you."

I had to admit that was a very good point. Maybe I was too trusting by nature. Did I trust Nigel? That was a hard question; it was not like triple-agents carried certificates of authenticity.

***

Needless to say, I tried to sleep that morning and into the afternoon, but it was a bust. Despite my late night out, I could never manage to get any kind of sleep with the sun up. Or was it the fact that I was learning the true definition of paranoia from a trained expert in the field? Maybe a little of both.

The cheap joint had lousy room service. For lunch, Nigel and I choked down stale sandwiches and drank warm beer.

"Pass the bottle, will you, Shawn?"

I handed him the beer, and he took a moment to fill his glass. "Too bad they never heard of refrigerators in this country," I said.

He looked up at me like I'd grown a second nose. "Whatever do you mean?"

"The beer. It's warm," I replied.

"Old man, that's the way they serve it here." He took another sip. "Rather good stuff actually. Reminds me of home."

"And where's home, Nigel?"

"Bath."

I blinked. "Huh? You just had a shower an hour ago."

"No, old man. The town, Bath. It's on the west coast of England. Charming little resort village. My father's family had a country house just south of town."

"Oh," I said, feeling a little stupid. "What did your pop do for a living?"

Nigel put down his half-empty glass on the nightstand and stared at it. "He was an officer in His Majesty's Royal Dragoons. Served in India on the Northwest Frontier, knighted into the 'Order of the St. Michel and St. George' in South Africa fighting the Boers. Wounded in France while leading a bayonet charge at the age of fifty-six; quite the hero, you know. He never won the Victoria Cross, but you'd think sometimes he was about to topple over from the weight of all the other medals he wore."

"Wow. My dad drove a milk wagon when he wasn't doing odd jobs."

Nigel nodded but made no reply. He never finished the beer. For the next hour, he ignored me and devoted his time to scribbling in a notebook. I tried to nap without much success. I kept trying to figure Nigel out. He seemed legit, and he certainly lived up to all his promises. But why did a man like him do the things, he did? He didn't seem very political, and certainly, there were safer ways to make a living than spying. My dad worked for Bugs when he didn't have a choice.

Did Nigel have a choice? I couldn't say.

The notebook shut with a snap as Nigel rose to his feet. "Well, old man, we need to get going, hmm."

"What's the plan?"

"You and I are going to go for a walk to reconnoiter the Charles Bridge. I want you to be standing over-watch while I do the brush-pass tomorrow morning."

"Wait, don't tell me. A brush-pass is where you slip something into another guy's mitt when you walk past him."

Nigel raised an eyebrow. "So you do have some training in tradecraft after all."

I shrugged. "Shooting the shit with my boss, Reynardie, back in Paris. He was the master spy, served in the OSS during the war. Me, I just listen good."

"Bravo. Actually, I'll be trading newspapers with my agent. I've folded my warning note into the one I'll give him, and he should have something for me as well."

"Too easy," I said.

***

The Charles Bridge was built by some king back in the days of knights and damsels, and they built it to last. Just six blocks from Old Town Square, it's about a hundred yards of fancy stonework with an honest to God castle at each end. I figured putting myself up in one of the castle towers would be a good spot for me to stand lookout, but Nigel pointed out that I'd have a hard time communicating with him from that distance. He also noted that if I got spotted, I'd have no place to run.

Instead, he suggested I do what I did so well back at the Guard De Nord train station in Paris. Namely, move around in a roving patrol and look for detectives. If I saw anybody suspicious, he wanted me to take off my hat and not put it back on. Sounded pretty simple to me, except I didn't like the hat part. It looked like it was going to rain.

***

As the fog swelled up from the Vltava River, I crossed the Charles Bridge at a slow walk. Nigel and I'd skipped breakfast that morning in favor of an early checkout from the grand Rat-Trap Hotel we had so recently called home. He described his next agent as a Russian army officer in his mid-fifties, about six foot two, with salt and pepper hair and a trim physique. Nigel told me to expect him to be in uniform, but that wasn't a sure thing. Like the last guy, this fellow was supposed to hold a newspaper in his right hand. I kept my eyes open.

The bridge was pretty crowded with commuters at that time of day. Folks on bicycles, on foot, and occasionally in cars or on motorcycles crossed in both directions under a heavy gray sky. The weather was definitely changing. I could see why Nigel picked this spot, however; it was easy to hide in the chaos. Unfortunately, that worked against me as much as it worked for him. I kept on the lookout for surveillance but in this mess, Bozo the Clown could walk right by me in full makeup, and I might not see him. Still, I stayed alert. People could die if I messed this up. People with families.

I spotted Nigel before I spotted his guy. Nigel wore his gray jacket with the collar pulled up and covered his perfect hair with a battered brown fedora. In his left hand, he carried a newspaper. I made like I'd forgotten something and crossed the street so I could double back. As I did, I passed a Red Army officer in a brown tunic and blue Bozo the Clown styled military trousers. In his right hand, he held a newspaper. I fumbled for a cigarette and dropped it on the sidewalk. That gave me a chance to look behind me, and it was worth the glance. One of the detectives I'd spotted at the tavern the other night kept pace about fifty feet behind Nigel's agent. I could hardly miss him; the moron wore the same double-breasted suit from the night before.

Nigel insisted we wore different outfits to every meet.

I stole a glance at Nigel. He was less than ten feet from the army officer and closing. There was no way he'd see my signal in time to abort the brush-pass. Shit.

I left the cigarette on the ground. My hand dove into my suit coat as I rose up. Closing with the detective in three quick strides, I blocked him cold in his tracks. He scowled at me with irritation as I drew from my coat pocket the map of Prague. With a smile, I said, "*An cluin thu mi mo nighean donn?*"

His face shifted to pure confusion, but I didn't let up. I opened the map and pointed at some random feature. "*Mi mo nighean donn?*"

What he said to me in Czech probably didn't count as anything polite, but that hardly mattered. What I said to him in Gaelic probably didn't make any sense. All I knew was that those were the words Grandpa Dullahan sang whenever he got drunk. By the time the thug shoved me aside, Nigel was walking past me with a different newspaper in his right hand.

***

The room service at our next hotel was much better. I knocked back a cup of high-class joe and spilled the last drop on my tie. "Nuts, I like this tie too."

Nigel looked up from his notebook. "Silk, hmm. Not that Yank nylon stuff. Put some water on it before the stain sets."

The bathroom smelled of lilacs and had these fancy soaps on the mantle. "Should I use hot water or cold?"

"I never was a washerwoman, old man. Use your own judgment." I flushed the tie with cold water and draped it over the towel rack. "Speaking of which, Shawn, what made you try your Gaelic with a Czech secret policeman?"

"Well," I emerged from the john and unbuttoned my shirt. "I figured if I tried any other language he'd either hear my American accent; or worse, he'd understand me. With Gaelic he'd just take me for some foreigner who he didn't have time for. Poor bastard's probably still trying to figure out what language he heard."

Nigel smiled. "Good point, old man. Like I keep saying, you've got fine instincts for this kind of work. I suppose you'll make it to the head of the American MI6 someday, hmm."

I tossed my shirt onto a chair and flopped down on our double bed. This hotel was out of rooms with single beds. "We don't have an MI6 or anything like that since Truman canned the OSS. There's some bunch in Washington called the Central Intelligence Group, or whatever, but I haven't heard much about 'em. I doubt I'd ever get too high up in anything like that, even if I wanted to. But I don't know. Maybe I could make this a career. If I don't get locked up at Fort Leavenworth first. By the way, that last guy, the Ruskie officer, did he have any cheddar for us?"

"Cheddar?"

"Information, Nigel. Did he have anything we could use?"

"That remains to be seen. All his note said was that I should go to our dead-drop. I expect he left a package for us there."

"And the note you wrote him," I asked, "what did it say?"

Nigel put his notebook down and rubbed his temples. "I told him to get the hell out of Czechoslovakia before it's too late."

"That gonna' be easy for him? Doesn't he have a family and all?"

"Nothing like this is ever easy," Nigel replied. "His family is back in Russia, and I don't know how, or if, they'll be able to get out. He has some money. I've paid him well over the years. With any luck, he sent some home and his wife will know whom to bribe. Dangerous business, old man."

I lit a cigarette. "So I've noticed."

***

The dead-drop was behind a loose stone in an old wall by the Strahov Monastery. Nigel didn't bother to tell me which stone exactly. "All I need you to do is walk past the wall and check for surveillance. If you see any, light a cigarette. Once the coast is clear, I'll retrieve the package and meet you back at the trolley stop where you did your first job for me."

"And then we find another second-story hotel room?"

"Exactly."

"You ain't worried that we're going to run out of hotels in Prague anytime soon, are you?"

He smiled at the thought. "No, Shawn. In fact, we should be leaving town the day after tomorrow. I only have one more agent to contact. Then we go our separate ways."

"I go west, and you go east." I clenched my teeth; somehow the thought of leaving him behind the Iron Curtain just didn't sit well with me.

"That's right, old man. We'll each go to meet our fate. Hopefully, you'll go with something to exonerate yourself."

"And what will you go with, Nigel?" I asked.

His answer was one word. "Redemption."

***

It wasn't exactly a stormy night, just pissing rain. An olive green top coat and Nigel's old brown hat gave me all the protection I needed from the elements; Nigel was a good shopper.

The old monastery was a huge whitewashed thing with onion domes on top of its steeples. Our destination...the old stone wall... just about a block away. I walked ahead, and Nigel was supposed to be far enough behind that he could just make out my silhouette. After I passed the stone wall my part was done.

The weather and the time of night collaborated with our little conspiracy; there weren't many people out at all. I tried to spot those detectives from before, but no. There was nobody like that on the street. I passed an old husband and wife that I wrote off as harmless, and in the distance, I could just make out a girl reading by a doorway light. But that was it, coast clear.

I kept walking. My cigarettes stayed in my pocket as I passed the dead-drop.

The trolley stop was easy to find. In only a few days' time, I'd gotten to know Prague pretty well despite its twisting, turning streets. Nigel joined me on the bench at five to two. "How did it go, buddy?" I asked.

"Not too bad." He patted his breast pocket. "My Russian friend gave us a thick envelope of Red Army telephone transcripts."

"What do they say?"

"Not so eager, old man. I haven't had time to do more than glance at them, and even so, they're in Russian. And Russian isn't in my repertoire."

"Sorry."

He was right, I was eager, but who could blame me for that? I was desperate to get something to clear me. Despite my misgivings about leaving Nigel behind, like any soldier in any war, I simply wanted to go home.

We got on the next trolley and spent an hour or so heading east into the city at a very slow pace. Not all of Prague was cathedrals and romantic buildings reflecting ancient glory. We passed through the factory side of town and beyond that the slum. Tenements replaced medieval towers as the city showed us it's seedier face. Eventually, we got off at a station that reeked of cheap booze and stale vomit. A lady of the evening in a yellow raincoat tried to entice us, but it was late, and her efforts were halfhearted.

Nigel seemed to know the neighborhood like the back of his hand. He took us straight to an old hotel with a green light illuminating its sign, and a second story room already reserved for him. The night clerk either knew Nigel well or was just in the habit of blowing a kiss at every guy he met.

Actually, the room wasn't half bad. It was bigger than most, and along with the usual double bed and nightstand, had a couch with a little coffee table. There were a few pictures on the wall, but none that would reveal anything beyond the taste of the resident. In the corner, a little kitchen with a dining table completed the room. "So, Nigel, this is your home away from home?"

"Yes, I'm afraid it is. This has been my base of operations for the past two years. You'll find some gin in the cupboard. Be a good man and hand me the bottle, please."

I obliged as he pulled a couple of shot glasses from the shelf. We toasted to nothing at all, and I shuddered at just how awful the stuff was. "Now what?"

"Now, my American friend, we get some rest. It's been a long day. Tonight I meet my last agent and give him the warning, as well as find out if he has anything of value to give us. When I get back, I'll write my final report, then give you my notebook for your return trip."

"Whoa there, buddy." This was a curveball, and out of left field at that. "What's this about you going to meet your agent and then coming back to me? Ain't I going along as your over-watch?"

"Not this time, Shawn. I simply don't need you."

That didn't jive with me. In two out of the last three meets, we'd encountered trouble. As cautious as Nigel was, it simply made no sense that he'd go solo on this one. "Bullshit, Nigel. What gives?"

He blinked rapidly. "Nothing. I simply don't need you along for this."

"Why not?"

His tone started to rise. "Well, if you must know I...." He must have seen the look on my face. He had started to get angry. It's a good way to throw most people off so they'll leave well enough alone. Liars use that tactic all the time. In a glance, he knew that wouldn't work on me, so he switched gears. "Shawn, I just would rather you didn't come. It's...well, it's embarrassing."

Embarrassing? What did that mean to a guy like Nigel? Now there was no way I was going to let him out of my sight. As Nigel himself said, you never know when you're going to be betrayed. Besides, if he was on the level, I needed to make sure this came out right. "Nigel, I'm seeing you safely on your way. That's part of a deal I made in church a few nights back. I do that, and I can walk into the stockade with my head held high. Otherwise, all this is for nothing."

He swallowed hard. "You're a good friend to me, Shawn."

I smiled and puffed up some Irish pride. "Just don't let that get around, limey. I've got a reputation to keep."

***

The rest of that day passed slowly. I took a nap, Nigel sipped gin and read a book called *Ivanhoe*. We opened up a couple of cans of hash for breakfast, lunch, and dinner. He didn't make any calls or go outside to draw any chalk circles on the pavement. I wondered about those Russian transcripts. Were they really in Russian, or did Nigel just want to keep them to himself? Maybe I was just nervous, but it was the first time he'd avoided sharing something with me that I'd asked for.

The meet put me off too. When I asked how he'd contact this last guy, Nigel just said, "Without any difficulty at all."

As answers go, that really stunk. But he wasn't saying anymore, and that rattled my cage. But what was I supposed to do? Take out my .45 and demand answers at gunpoint? If Nigel had been playing me all this time it was way too late to just back out and go home. Or was it? Even if I did arrest him, how the hell would I get him back to American custody from Prague, Czechoslovakia? Despite his silence, my options were quite limited. If I didn't like it that was simply too bad for me. So I gave up on it and ate another can of hash. After four cans of the stuff, I wasn't looking forward to my next trip to the john. But like my faith in Nigel, if things just around the bend went bad I'd just have to deal with it.

An hour past sunset, Nigel announced it was time to go.

"Shouldn't we do a reconnaissance first?" I asked him as I donned a brown suit coat.

"Not this time, old man. It's a pretty straightforward affair. I'm meeting my agent in a hotel where he does business of a sort. The police never set foot inside, and there is only the one street entrance and a fire escape in the side alley. Either exit is visible from the café directly across the street. Once I'm in the hotel, you'll have no way of contacting me. However, I will look out the window before I leave to see if you're still at the café. If I see you, I'll know it's safe to come out. If I don't, I will assume ambush awaits and will take necessary precautions. Once our business is done, I'll meet you at the train station, give you my notebook and any other information I have, and say goodbye."

Sounded too easy. That had me worried. "You sure you can see me in the café?"

"No doubt there. The café is a street affair, like the one we used back in Berlin the day you arrested that American girl. Ghellers, I think her name was?"

"Gillars," I corrected him. That brought back memories. Had I actually known Nigel that long? "So when this is over, it's all over. The whole damn shooting match?"

"I'm afraid so, Shawn." Reaching in his wallet, he gave me a wad of dough. "That's for a drink at the café, and it will also cover your travel expenses if we don't reconnect." He snuffed out his cigarette on the dining table and stuck out his hand. "Whatever comes, it's been a pleasure to serve with you."

We gave each other a firm clasp. Then I got my things together—shoulder holster, coat, hat, and coffee stained silk tie—and followed him out the door.

He stopped me, "That's the same coat you wore last night, Shawn."

I looked down at my topcoat. "It's the only overcoat I have."

"Best to go without, I'm afraid."

"You're the boss." I shrugged off the coat and draped it over the couch, never to see it again.

We emerged into the early evening twilight to a drizzling rain. The weather didn't keep folks indoors, not in this neighborhood. There was business to be done. On just about every corner were small clusters of girls in brightly colored raincoats. Below the yellow, blue, and red slickers, I saw short skirts and long legs with fishnet stockings. Like I said, there was business to be done.

Nigel and I got approached once. Otherwise, the girls were content to holler and wave as we passed. However, as we turned the corner and headed for the hotel, even the most persistent gave up on us. I went left and Nigel went right. On the left side of the street lay the brightly lit café, a nice little place with a yellow and red striped awning and a collection of mismatched chairs and tables. I took a seat at a battered old table and watched Nigel head up the stairs and into the hotel across the street. A few men stood outside under the easement and watched him go in. One wore an apricot scarf and the other had his peach shirt unbuttoned down to his navel. The colors suited 'em well, as I was pretty sure each one was a fruit.

A waiter came for my order, but I just pantomimed a cup of tea. He shrugged and walked away. When he returned, he gave me a glass of wine with an indifferent look. I paid him, not even sure if I just barely covered the cost or gave him one whopper of a tip. But it didn't matter at all. I was there for Nigel and nothing else.

I had just taken my first sip from the glass when out of the corner of my eye I saw a prostitute in a red Mackintosh walking toward the café. I've got to admit, I didn't pay her much attention. She looked nothing like a detective and therefore couldn't be a threat. Then she ducked under the striped awning and came straight for my table.

"Hello, Shawn. Is nice evening, no?"

Holy Mary, Mother of God! Romana had just sat down next to me.

CHAPTER ELEVEN

Romana fixed me with a steady gaze and an inviting smile. I was floored, but not entirely at a loss for words.

"No." I blinked rapidly for a couple of seconds before I could focus on her question. Excess makeup and a racy outfit didn't hide her natural beauty. She was radiant, a beautiful distraction that forced concentration to come late into my noggin. "I mean, yes. It is a nice evening." A clap of thunder rang out in the night sky, proving to the world, and Romana, what a liar I was. "What the hell are you doing here?"

In mock indignation, she gasped. "Such language!" She leaned in. "Maybe I just wanted to see you?"

Regaining some composure, I answered, "I doubt it. By the way, you left something in your trunk."

"Yes." She nodded. "I thought you could do a comrade a favor."

My eyes narrowed. "And the reason you couldn't have told this comrade in advance?"

The waiter arrived before she could answer. Speaking to him in rapid Czech, she pointed to me and he soon departed. "Shawn, you tell me Nigel trained you. If so, body of poor Otto not problem. If you lied to me, I would soon be reading of arrest for murder of western spy in papers. It was test."

"And I passed?"

"Yes, obviously," she replied. "I also check your story with friend in American army. You are in a lot of trouble, comrade deserter. And even more interesting, they are now looking for a special agent who aided in escape of spy from Berlin jail. Would you know who person is?"

"Yes, I would," I answered. "I told you, I'm trying to help our friend, Nigel."

She looked at me for a long moment. "Is Nigel our friend? Do you trust?"

Good question. By way of stalling, I simply answered, "I've known him for a long time."

Romana pressed, "And you trust?"

"I suppose." Needing to know what she was getting at, I added, "He hasn't betrayed me or the party."

At that she crossed her arms and asked, "What did he tell you?"

"You're asking an awful lot of questions, Romana. My turn. What's going on?"

Before she could answer, the waiter returned with a glass of wine for her. Again she pointed at me, and I paid him with the same denomination as before. He flashed a big smile; I must've been a great tipper.

"I am rude, no?" She raised her glass. "To special friends. You and I."

We let the glasses clink.

"So," I smiled, "we are still friends?"

"Oh, yes, Shawn. Have you missed me?" Her raincoat parted to reveal that succulent bosom in a low cut black dress. Lovely, but not enough to get me completely off track.

I hedged back into the conversation on the easiest path I could find. "I've missed you." With a sly grin, I added, "We had a wonderful time in Frankfort. Nigel's a good traveling companion. But sharing a hotel room with you would make things a lot more comfortable."

A giggle escaped her lips, causing a bubbly storm in the little sea of her wine glass. "You have shared hotel with Nigel? Have you one bed or two?"

"Uh, both," I answered. "We've moved around a lot. Why?"

Her smile slid sideways. "I did not think you were his type, is all."

"What are you getting at, Romana?"

"Nigel, he likes boys. You not know?"

My jaw dropped. Nigel had seen me undress. He'd slept in the same bed as me more than once and never tried anything funny. "Bullshit."

Leaning back in her chair, she regarded me with amused eyes. "Shawn, what do you think Nigel is doing in hotel across street now? Is bordello, yes? But have you seen girls?"

My eyes turned back to the two guys outside the door of the place. Boy, was I stupid. But Nigel a fairy? "He told me he was a commando in the war, cut men's throats with a dagger."

"Yes," she replied. "He taught me to do. Is how poor Otto died. But why can such a man not like boys? His secret was finally found out. Is why MI6 dismissed him. Is why there is warrant for his arrest in England for crime of homosexuality."

Well—that was a surprise. By Romana's amused expression, my face looked like one of those cartoon characters that just got hit with a frying pan.

I'd had no clue Nigel was a pansy, and I couldn't have guessed. He'd lied to me about working for MI6's Twenty Division! My brain got temporarily disconnected, and all I could do was repeat the obvious back to her. "Nigel was fired from MI6?"

"Yes," She nodded. "Is why he offered to defect. He claimed to be one who gave us names of Berlin scientist back in '46, for reason he wanted both sides balanced. Nigel told that he thought world scary place with only Americans having bomb. But he now felt 'stabbed in back' by king and country for dismissal, and would do anything to hurt capitalist betrayers. Or perhaps he just feared being discovered as NKVD's Berlin man someday, and thought it better to switch sides while he could. Then again, maybe he's just greedy? Is perhaps why he asked party for so much money. Confusing man, Nigel Leer."

Well, now I knew how Nigel bankrolled our little vacation. I let that sink in. It took a while. Romana just sipped her wine and stared at me. This could have all been part of Nigel's triple-agent cover story. The reason he gave the Russians for trusting him so he could begin his assignment. But then again, he was throwing a lot of cash around, and the hotel clerk recognized him.

He'd blown Nigel a kiss.

No doubt, she knew I was off balance and pressed her advantage. "You have known him long? You say he taught you to be discreet back in Berlin. We had source in MI6 back then. We never saw his face, very careful person, used dead-drops only. Nigel claims that it was him, but we cannot confirm. Can you confirm?"

My lie came automatically and gave me a springboard to jump back on the offensive. "Yes. I'm a counterintelligence man. That means my job is to catch spies. I discovered Nigel but didn't report him. That's when we became friends. But why are you here now? You said you had a job to do in the East for the party. Is this that job?"

She hesitated, but she seemed to know if she wanted information from me, she'd have to give some in return. "We have another comrade in MI5 who gave us list of capitalist agents working in Prague. When he came to us, Nigel gave exact same list to NKVD. Is why we believed him. I was sent to work surveillance team to watch these traitors, but is no good. They put me with bunch of dummies in fancy suits who think they are professionals. They call themselves secret police but cannot keep secret from shoeshine boy. Everybody knows who they are. I am only girl who works with them, so I get shit jobs. They even take my gun. They try to tail western spies and end up chasing own tails while I do filing. So I work on my own now."

"And you're here because...."

"Because, Shawn Riggs, in hotel across street is one of Nigel's old agents. One he supposedly betrayed to us. And you know who is with this capitalist son-of-bitch right now?"

"Nigel," I volunteered. Why hide it? By this point she knew or we wouldn't be talking. But by confirming that, was I turning Nigel in? Okay, so she suspected Nigel wasn't a Communist after all, but I had to know what she thought of me. Was I still her Bolshevik brother, or was she now wondering about the best way to slit my throat and shove me in a car trunk?

"Yes, our good friend, comrade Leer. So I ask, what did Nigel tell you?"

I started with the truth and worked my way out from there. "He told me he was going east. He needed to escape. He told me I'd been betrayed and if I didn't defect with him, I'd be sent to Fort Leavenworth." She tilted her head. "That's a special prison in America. I don't want to go to prison, so I'm traveling with him. He wants to introduce me to his NKVD handler. Maybe this guy can send me back to America with a new identity."

"Shawn, remember, I check on you. You are deserter, yes, is true. But NKVD has no knowledge of you giving party information or offering to defect."

"I never gave the party information," I answered. "All I did was make sure good Communists weren't found out. Goddamn it, Romana! I let one guy go just a day before I got word that they were after Nigel. Go ahead, check that out if you can, and you'll see I'm on the level."

"Hmm." She seemed to be buying my story, but I was still sweating. She mulled it over, then asked, "And what happened to Venediktov and Bezrukov?"

"Who?" I asked.

"Venediktov and Bezrukov, two comrades heading west. Were supposed to meet Nigel. Have not been seen since."

Well, now I knew Igor and Peter's last names, but had no idea which name belonged to who. Honesty is the best policy sometimes, so I simply answered her question the way she asked it. "I never heard of either of those names before, and Nigel never brought up any guys like that to me."

She held out her hand and clasped mine across the table. "Shawn, you are in over head. Nigel lied to you, yes?"

I nodded.

"I not know what kind of game he plays," she continued. "But he was at secret place last night. I saw him get package from wall that was left by treasonous Red Army soldier. That soldier now is disappeared. Maybe he defect to West? What do you know about this?"

"Nothing," I lied. "Was Nigel alone, or are there others I need to watch out for?"

She answered, "I saw few people—an old couple out for walk maybe, and a few passersby in overcoats—but no one with him."

Well, shit, that meant I did my job half-right last night. Romana hadn't spotted me, but I'd failed to spot her. That left Nigel flapping in the wind. Some over-watch I was.

To delay her next question I threw a random one at her. "Is Nigel dangerous?"

A short laugh escaped her lips. "Of course. He British commando, remember? But I don't think he kill you. Maybe you his pretty boy?"

I sat up straighter. "Now hold on here—"

"Shawn," she interrupted, "I make sure Nigel not a threat. Then, I let you meet my handler at NKVD. We maybe can get you to America with new name. You can work for party in hometown of Chicago."

So, she still thought I was from Chicago. I'd forgotten I'd told her that lie. I didn't answer her, just stared into my wine like I was thinking about it.

She pressed on. "I remember you side with workers, like your father."

Well, at least that part wasn't entirely a lie. It just meant something different to me than it did to her. "How are you going to stop Nigel?"

Now it was her turn not to answer me. I asked, "Are you going to arrest him?"

"Me? Alone? No, would be stupid. I get fancy suits to do. Make them useful for change."

That made sense, but I needed to know more. "What do you want me to do, Romana?" I let my eyes return to her beautiful breasts and linger there. "I want to help you."

She thought it over and took another sip of wine. "You stay with Nigel, keep an eye. Do not let him get spooked. I come back with fancy suits in few hours."

"And when these fancy suits come, they come for Nigel, not me, right?"

She let go of my hand as her eyes shifted to her glass. "Of course."

Now she was back to lying to me. For some strange reason, that made me feel more comfortable. "Romana, I've run this far to stay out of an American prison. I don't need to end up in a Russian one. Tell me that the men will know I'm a comrade."

"The men will know you're a comrade." She answered my question just the way I asked it. Cute, Romana.

It was my turn to press her, shake her tree and see what fell loose. "Let me guess. They'll arrest me too, and ship my ass off to Siberia."

"No." She shook her head. "You will see. Why would they want to arrest you?"

"Because I'm an American counterintelligence agent, and things aren't too rosy between America and the people's government just now. To your fancy suit friends, I'm just a pawn. Someone for you to use and throw away."

"Shawn, we all must sacrifice," she said. "But we need you. You can be a great service to party."

"To the party. But am I still just a pawn to you?"

Her eyes flared as she shot up in her seat. "Shawn! How dare you? I'm your friend. Your special friend, remember? If you not trust me now, after all have done, well, I—"

"It's okay, I'm sorry, Romana. I've just been through a lot these past few days." She calmed down right away, her anger fading just slowly enough to convince most folks it was real. But it wasn't real, and I knew it. Liars always get mad at the beginning when they're caught. I'd hit the nail right on the goddamned head.

"You go," I told her. "I'll stay and watch Nigel. He has an apartment two blocks that way." I pointed the direction we'd come from. "In an old hotel with a green light out front. His room is on the second floor. I'll keep him there until the cops arrive."

She nodded slowly, cautiously. My answer was what she wanted, but it came a little too quickly. She'd finally caught me in a lie.

For a moment she just stared at me.

"Is good, Shawn. I go now." She didn't even finish her wine as she rose from the table and left the café.

I watched as she ducked her head under the awning, rainwater splashing in her wake. Watching that slender, lovely form in the red raincoat walk away reminded me how lovely she looked. Of course, the ugly thing was she was walking straight into the arms of the secret police. Romana once asked me whose side I was on. Not the side of the people responsible for a town like Stieglitz, not the side behind the housewife's wooden smile. After all, I was still a sergeant in the US Army. I needed to do a good job, and there was no way in hell I could let her turn my buddy in.

When she was a block away, I got up and followed her into the rain. There was no polishing, no stealth. She saw me and I didn't expect otherwise. I took a final glance at the hotel brothel, not sure if Nigel saw me leave. But that wasn't so important right then. She knew we were no longer sweethearts.

Romana dodged around a corner; I picked up my pace and rounded it as the rain seeped into my brown coat. The green top coat would have come in handy just then, but Nigel had said no, and I'd trusted him. Despite his lies, I couldn't have traveled with a guy like Nigel for a week without discovering a few truths about him. Now that I knew the rest of his story, the pieces came together. It all made perfect sense.

    She trotted across the street, and I trotted after her. Her head swirled around frantically, but there were no crowds, no lighted windows, and no rescue to be seen. She'd made a wrong turn. This was the bad part of town, with nothing but boarded windows, abandoned doorways, and dark shadows. There'd be no help for her here. It was just Romana, and the rain, and me.

    For a while, she stuck to the sidewalks where the occasional streetlight may have given her some comfort. She knew I wouldn't grab her in the light. I needed the dark to…to do I didn't know what. Could I catch her? And if I did, how could I keep her from the cops? My mind raced, trying to think of a way. There had to be a way.

    Glancing frequently over her shoulder, she dodged around the neighborhood to no avail. She found every dead end as she darted around, going in circles. My bet was that in her days of filing for the fancy suits, she hadn't learned the streets. As for me, I'd learned the method behind Prague's madness, and the twisting, turning streets no longer baffled me. Too bad for her.

    Romana took a quick left, and I could hear the sudden pounding of her heels on the pavement as she ran in earnest. I took off at a sprint and rounded the corner in time to catch a glimpse of her red coat darting into an alleyway. Was she getting away? Would that get me off the hook? Not likely.

    My feet splashed puddles left and right as I made for that alley at a dead run. I had to stop her or people would die, people with families; Nigel and I among them. My hand went into my suit coat to grasp the handle of my .45 and the gun came out.

    As I turned into the alley, the smell of wet garbage assaulted my nose from the bins scattered about. But as my nose recoiled, my eyes focused on the wooden fence that stood at least a yard higher than her head at the alley's far end. Thank God, I thought; I had her now. With her trapped, maybe I could detain her until I found Nigel. He was the master spy; he'd know what to do. I wanted someone to tell me I didn't have to do what it looked like I might do. I wanted that very much. But in this neighborhood, there was no help for me either.

Romana stopped halfway to the fence and spun to face me. The rain had smeared her mascara into a mask of terror. Her eyes locked with mine, so full of fear there wasn't room for anything else. But I wasn't there to bring her pity. I had to end this somehow.

Her eyes cast down to my hand, where she saw my gun. Her gaze shifted up to lock with mine. Then with the speed of a star athlete, she spun around and sprinted for the fence. I thought this was going to be easy; I'd just tackle her against the boards and then...what? I wasn't sure. I didn't want to think about what might come next.

Suddenly, the gypsy girl took flight in an amazing leap. Her feet stumbled over a trash can as her hands grasped the top of the fence. With a heave, she catapulted over it in one bound. A second later she was over and gone.

Pure momentum took me to the fence, where I stopped cold. But it was an old fence and missing boards. I could see her running across a vacant lot at full tilt. But I could also see she was tired...soon she'd need to rest. The first bullet caught her between the shoulder blades, the second in the small of her back.

She didn't scream. Through my gun-sights, I watched her stagger on a few steps before collapsing in the mud with a sickening splat.

I busted out a few loose boards and crossed the lot to where she lay. Her face was planted in mud, tilted slightly to her left. Out of her nose and mouth, a red froth gushed, foaming around her head. Her shoulders rose and fell in an erratic, painful motion that was too terrible to watch, and surely worse to experience. Romana's death rattle came an eternity later.

The rain continued to bead up on her shiny red coat but didn't seem able to wash away the blood that pooled around her angelic form.

CHAPTER TWELVE

I walked away, my suit soaking wet and my heart torn into small, jagged pieces. Goddamn it! Why the hell did she have to show up? Why the hell did she have to know so much? Why the hell did she have to be so beautiful…and tragic?

When I passed a storm drain my gun took a swan dive, never to be seen again by the eyes of man. Let them flog me for losing it. I didn't give a fuck.

I didn't take the trolley; I walked to the train station. It gave me time to think, but my thoughts wouldn't stay together. Romana's last moments were seared into my mind, and I needed to somehow get them out. Looking for an escape, my mind went to Nigel's story, the truth behind his lies.

It made sense now, and I could walk in his shoes. His father, a hero of his nation. His mother, his nation's enemy. He'd joined the commandos to show to everyone he was taking his father's side for king and country. To prove that he was his father's son he needed to play the war hero. But war heroes kill people, and he didn't like that.

Easy for me to understand; it seemed I didn't like killing either.

But I was alive and had other things to think about. I figured after the commandos, Nigel chose to serve his country in a way that better suited his talents. Telling lies and keeping secrets most likely came naturally to a guy like him; after all, he'd kept one big dark secret all his life.

By the time I got to the train station the sun had breached the horizon. The air slowly grew warm and moist as sunny sky assaulted damp pavement. The storm had passed and hot weather was returning to Czechoslovakia. My legs felt like old tree stumps, and my suit looked like a collection of dishrags stitched together. Now I knew everything. But I didn't want to care about anything;

not about Nigel, not about the army, and especially, I didn't want to care about Romana. I didn't want to, but I did.

Walking into that magnificent place, I looked up to see those same statues of ancient saints staring at me. Their gaze turned from comfort to judgment, and I bore it as my due. Nevertheless, Nigel waited for me by the ticket window, his face a portrait of sorrow.

"I saw you leave after Romana from the café."

I didn't answer him. Not because I was mad. He lied to me, sure, but he had his reasons. Rejected and humiliated despite his years of loyal service, Nigel was a man who couldn't go home. But oddly he wasn't bitter…he was still his father's son; a loyal subject, and a hero for king and country. But I was simply too exhausted to speak. I said nothing.

To my silence, he replied, "I went looking for you two."

Of course, he did.

Nigel paused. "I found her body."

I looked at my shoes, filthy with mud.

He said, "It's a dangerous business, old man."

"So I've noticed." I took a good long look at my friend, and oddly enough, I now considered him closer to me than anyone else on Earth. "You lied to me, Nigel."

His face twitched into a smile as if warming up to pitch another whopper. But before the wind-up, he dropped the ball. "I did," he nodded. "I never met John Masterman. MI6 didn't send me on this mission."

"I know."

"Shawn, I am still who I say I am. I'm going to find out who that traitor in MI5 is and expose the bastard if it's the last bloody thing I ever do! The only way I can do that now is from inside the NKVD."

"Because there's a warrant for your arrest in Britain."

His eyes cast down. "I never meant to break the law. I never had so much as a tryst in my own country. But to be…what I am, is a crime in itself." He looked up, eyes filled with pain. "I've tried, Shawn. Oh dear God, have I tried. But I've never fancied women, and I can't help being what I am."

His tone was desperate. Desperate to be understood, to be respected or just to be accepted. I didn't know how to comfort him. I was dealing with too much myself just then. I only stared at him, and he'd have to read in my face what he would.

After apparently reaching some conclusion about me I'd never know, he nodded and reached into his suit pocket. "I bought your ticket to Berlin. Your train leaves at nine this morning, platform two."

I accepted the ticket without a word.

Opening his jacket, he produced the notebook and the envelope of Russian dispatches. "I didn't get much from my last man. He could only say that certain Red Army units have moved west to support the blockade of Berlin. His sources were among the soldiers that departed, and they are no longer patronizing the hotel."

"Brothel," I corrected.

"Yes, that too."

We stared at each other for a long moment, both of us knowing we would never see the other again. I had exposed him as a liar and a homosexual, but I was the one who had just murdered a woman in cold blood. We were both as reprehensible as men could be, but neither of us could help that. It was the very nature of the business we were in.

Nigel and I didn't say goodbye. He turned, I turned, and we went our separate ways. Maybe he would find his redemption. But I doubted I ever would.

***

I didn't sleep, and I didn't eat. My eyes just lazily surveyed the scenery as the antique locomotive rumbled west. Some of Nigel's gin would've gone down good just then, so I got up and walked to the dining car. I was in luck…the steward spoke English, but my good fortune ended there.

"What the hell do you mean there's no booze?"

In slow, deliberate English, the dining car guy explained. "Sir. We have none. We did have...much. But the last train was all...was all Russian soldiers. We have none."

"Great."

I stomped back to my seat in the passenger car, my head screaming with the onset of a migraine. Shivering in my wet clothes, I figured hypothermia wouldn't be far behind. Too bad for me. Thinking a smoke would warm me up, I checked my pockets, but that was a bust too. My cigs were as soaked as my socks, and you'd need a flamethrower to light either of 'em. The only thing mostly dry was Nigel's notebook and the envelope of Russian Army transcripts.

I looked left, I looked right.

Nobody sat by me and the guy in the next row over snored like a broken jackhammer. Opening the notebook, I took a gander at Nigel's reports. Frankly, they didn't make much sense. All the names of people and places were replaced with codes: *5670 reports three 13s of the RA to be deploying N of Sparrow in preparation for possible A84. 5670 could provide no additional information on RA units to remain in Sparrow at this time...* Riveting reading, Nigel; I can't wait 'til they publish the paperback.

The notebook went back into my breast pocket and out came the envelope. Like Nigel said, it was in Russian. What Nigel had failed to mention was that his agent had provided a note, in English, at the back. It read:

From the conversation between Zhukov and Konev of June 19^{th,} it seems apparent that any attempt by the West to supply Berlin by land will be met with military force. If the West decides to abandon the city, however, such Allied troops will be allowed to leave with only a Soviet military escort. Interestingly, Zhukov stated that any attempt to supply Berlin by air will not be opposed. According to him, Comrade Stalin directed Soviet forces to respect *the agreement of 30 November 1945 regarding the three air corridors. It is thus possible that key personnel can be evacuated. At this time, I would like to include my family among such personnel. They have been living in the eastern quarter of Berlin for the past few weeks, and I have instructed my wife to meet with the British Consulate as soon as possible. Please, expect her and do not turn her, or my children, away. I am being watched and expect to be disappeared any day now. For the sake of all I have done for my British friends, I beg you, please not to turn my family away.*

Of course, it wasn't signed, and there was no mention of the names of this guy's wife or kids. Was this written by that Russian army officer I saw on the bridge or someone he handled? I had no way of finding out. But regardless of my ignorance, someone at MI6 would know who this joker was, and his family too. He'd have a code name like 2345, or maybe something neat like Firebrand, and in some file would be his real name, his family's names, and a whole write up.

Fine, I'd do right by this guy. I'd get the envelope to the boys in Army G2. They'd make sure it got to the right people in MI6. If his family hadn't been caught yet, there'd still be a fair chance they could hop a flight to England—maybe even get to Bath. At least somebody could escape this whole fucked up mess.

I knew I sure as hell wouldn't.

***

The train arrived in Berlin at the Friedrichstrasse train station, Russian side of town. It was a busy place. People hustled and bustled beneath the steel girdered arches, and packed the two slender platforms. However, my eyes focused on the one thing that really mattered; on every corner and every exit stood one of those comrades in uniform. Long lines formed from the trains to the gates, each one ending in a bright young man from Leningrad ready to check your papers.

There wasn't much of a choice. To stand anywhere but in line meant putting a spotlight on myself. My heart pounded, and I broke out in a sweat, my head throbbing and my body shivering as I shuffled forward with the crowd of strangers one by one. Standing on the platform, waiting my turn to get nabbed, my mind raced for an out, but I couldn't think of one.

I sneezed.

Not surprising, my suit was still damp and I'd gotten the chills hours ago. Lacking a hanky my sleeve had to suffice; not the manners Mrs. Riggs would approve of. Folks backed off and gave me some room—a lot of room. I've got to admit; I was slow to figure out why. After all, I was just some wet, sweaty stranger who obviously had the shakes, spewing his contamination all over a crowded platform.

Why should they be worried?

As I neared the end of the line, I just let my body do what it wanted. I was breathing hard, coughing, shaking, and using my coffee-stained tie to wipe the sweat off my brow. When the Russian kid in the brown uniform challenged me, I let out a violent cough as I rummaged through my coat for papers I didn't have.

"*Privyet...,*" the soldier began. However, he soon fell silent as he gawked at this dreadful apparition. "*Privyet*, comrade...," he tried to continue, but it was no use. I let out a terrible sneeze that left snot dangling over my upper lip.

By the time I'd finished performing that spectacle, the poor kid just waved me past. I gave him a polite nod. But the soldier turned away, obviously trying his best to put me out of his mind already.

Welcome to Berlin's Russian Sector, Shawn, me lad.

As I shuffled past the kid, I heard a shout. No matter the army, no matter the language, you can always recognize a sergeant's bellowing. A pudgy excuse for a non-commissioned officer shouted at the kid and pointed at me. Shit! The gig was up. Taking to my heels, I bolted for the first exit I saw, a wide-open stairway that led down. People shouted in German, Russian, and maybe a few other languages all blended together. But even though all the commotion, I could clearly hear the sound of a bolt being jacked back in a rifle.

"*Ostanovka!*" was the last word I heard before the wet slap of a bullet raced past my ear. To my right, a yellow tile exploded, and I could now add another Russian word to my limited foreign vocabulary.

The stairs led to a dark subway platform. The only working lights were clustered around construction equipment in this dank, abysmal place. The half dozen workers took one look at me and raised their hands. Obviously, they had enough problems without borrowing mine. A whistle blew and the six guys dove for cover. I turned to see an equal number of soldiers barreling down the stairway right after me.

There was light up ahead and I sprinted for it, all the while my head throbbing and my lungs coughing up whatever was left of my self-respect. I got maybe ten feet from that light and was just about to bolt up those stairs when another whistle blew from up top. More shouts in Russian and more cocking of rifles directly above me. Shit!

Spinning in place, I slipped on the tiles and landed chin first on the floor. Booted footsteps closed in as I opened a bleary eye to see Sergeant Fatso of the People's Army rushing my way. I rolled off the platform and onto the tracks, my feet hitting the ground without a pause before running again. Running like my life depended on it—because it did—I beat feet into the dark train tunnel. I couldn't see one foot in front of my face, and that turned out to be a good thing. That darkness must have saved my skin as bullets skipped off the tunnel's walls and steel tracks around me. Somewhere my left shoe caught on something soggy and, for all I know, it's still on those tracks today.

After a while, the shouting and the shooting stopped, but I kept running. Just because I couldn't see them didn't mean the

Ruskies weren't there. I tried to be quiet about it, but it was a real effort to keep my breathing and coughing down in the musky air.

Where were they now? I looked behind me and all I could see was dark. What would I do if I were a Russian flat-foot? I'd station a guard at the Friedrichstrasse station and call ahead to have another squad waiting for me at the end of the line. What was I going to do about that? The only thing that occurred to me was prayer, but after shooting a girl in the back, I had no right to expect the Holy Saints to intervene on my sorry behalf. Maybe this was His punishment after all? I thought murder was the first on the list of seven deadly. Yeah, that would make sense. Why else would the Church have a list of seven "deadly" sins if murder wasn't at the top? Would God forgive murder? Did I want Him to? Damn me, I sure as hell didn't deserve any better from the Almighty.

And yet, a light shone from above.

Rounding a bend, I saw a single shaft of light piercing the tunnel about twenty yards ahead. Twisted wires and bent girders dangled around the hole. A shell hole, about a yard and a half around, gaped to the right side of the tunnel. War damage, waiting to be repaired.

Thank you, Lord.

It wasn't easy, but I managed to jump high enough to grab a steel pipe on the third try, then pull myself up and into the sunlight. Crawling out, I looked around. The late afternoon sun shone hot on the pavement I was hugging. Not too many folks were on the street and the ones that were pretended not to look at me. My filthy, wet, single shoed appearance did everything it could to keep decent people away. Hell, I bet even the pickpockets wouldn't dirty their hands on a bum like me.

Time to get walking.

The bright sunshine helped dry my suit out but only made my headache worse. Adding to the fun, I didn't have a map of Berlin, and this part of town was completely unfamiliar to me. I wandered around for hours, not sure if I was going east or west. I tried asking directions a few times with my scraps of German. It didn't do much good, although one kind soul did tell me where to find a toilet.

Looking at myself in the mirror gave no encouragement. My chin was swollen where it had hit the concrete. My left foot bled some, and just then my biggest fear was tetanus or whatever plague dwelled in abandoned German subways. I washed my cuts in cold tap water using an old, wrinkled up bar of soap. At least I exited the john somewhat cleaner than I went in. Now I just looked like a bum, not a bum with leprosy.

It was getting near sunset when I found the checkpoint. On one side of Zimmerstrabe Street sat a squad of Soviet troops on a pile of sandbags, smoking cigs and staring at a few American dog faces in a Jeep across the way. The Americans were living in relative style; they had a card table and some folding chairs. The Russians stopped every car and truck that passed their way and searched it, but they paid no attention to the pedestrians who shuffled past. That would do for me. I walked right past 'em without as much as a "by your leave."

Stopping by the Jeep, I asked the GI with the sword and rainbow patch, "Hey, Mack, where's your higher located?"

He squinted his eyes at me and made a visible effort not to breathe through his nose. "Who wants to know?"

I reached in my pocket and discreetly flashed him my badge, whispering, "Special Agent Riggs, US Army Counterintelligence Corps."

The guy's eyes about bugged out of his sockets, but he was smart enough not to draw the Russian's attention. "I'll radio my sergeant. He can give you a ride to our HQ."

"Thanks." I was just starting to feel lucky when I looked down to see the bumper numbers on his Jeep, *D/2-6 INF.*

That's when I knew I was truly fucked, but there was nothing for it. I waited to meet my fate. When the Jeep arrived, I met a staff sergeant who was a little wary of letting a hobo into his nice, clean vehicle, but he was otherwise friendly. From there we took a short ride to the now familiar to me McNair Army Barracks; the tower clock read 1900 hours.

The place lacked the hustle and excitement I'd seen on my last visit. Troops walked around unarmed, some with their hands in their pockets. I saw a few machine gun nests around the perimeter. The soldiers behind those .30 calibers were smoking and joking. The blockade of Berlin was becoming normal.

The staff sergeant led me into the white brick complex, and through a series of twists and turns, we ended up in the headquarters office of D Company. The plain wood office door bore a cartoon with a bulldog on a chain and read, "Welcome to the dog house." Cute.

It was a standard layout; a few beat-up desks in a common room clustered with bulletin boards. Some doors that led to some smaller offices were off to the side. A skinny lieutenant sat on a desk with a magazine in his hand and a cigarette in his mouth. He looked me up and down and didn't seem at all impressed. "What ya' got there, Sergeant?"

"Sir, this man approached the checkpoint at Friedrichstrasse and Zimmerstrabe. Says he's an FBI Agent."

"Counterintelligence Agent," I corrected the staff sergeant. "My name is Shawn Riggs, I'm a Special Agent with the US Army's Counterintelligence Corps Team 4. I need to see your company's S2 right away."

"Uh, I'm the Officer Of the Day," the lieutenant replied. "Can I help?"

"Lieutenant, you got a top secret clearance and a need to know clandestine information?"

He shook his head.

"I didn't think so." Looking around, I saw what I needed most and grabbed a box of tissues off a desk. My nose trumpeted loud and long; nothing more disgusting than black boogers. "I haven't had a very good day, Lieutenant. Just get me your intelligence officer, now."

Dog Companies' intelligence officer was a friendly guy named Captain Fredrick who offered me a cup of coffee. It was terrible; I was back in the army all right. As a bonus he let me bum a cigarette. A long day without and already I had the shakes. I knew I had never felt better in my life than when I took a drag of that sweet smoke, and it actually felt for a moment like things were going to be all right.

Once the skinny lieutenant shut the door and we were alone in Fredrick's office, he asked, "What can I do for you, Agent Riggs?"

Pulling a cheap wooden chair up to his desk, I took a seat and rubbed my sore left foot. "You got any aspirin, Sir?"

"Why, yes, I do." He reached into his drawer, and I gulped down four of 'em in one go.

"Thanks, Sir."

He gave me a puzzled, "You're welcome."

My hand went into my coat pocket, and out came the notebook. "These are reports by a British MI6 agent named Nigel Leer. He's believed to be a defector, but he's actually running an offensive operation against the Communists from behind Russian lines. This is all hot stuff, so I'd appreciate it if you'd get one of your intel clerks to start typing it up so we can send it up the chain, pronto."

Reverently, he took the notebook. "I see. I've got some good men under me, Agent, and they all had their clearances updated last month. We'll see this gets handled right."

I nodded and took another sip of the wretched coffee. "I got something else for you." Reaching into another pocket produced the envelope. "Soviet military transcripts of high-level phone conversations. I'm not sure what most of them mean 'cause they're in Russian. But I do know one guy's hoping this information is worth the lives of his wife and kids. He's probably dead right now.

However, his family is in Berlin and they're going to try for the British Consulate. I need you to see that G2 lets the Brits know to expect 'em."

"Well, I…."

"Captain, the information I just dropped in your lap cost some people their lives." I stared at him for a good long minute and watched his eyes turn from confusion to resolve.

"You have my word, Agent. It will be done."

"Good." I didn't tell him that the life lost belonged to a couple of thugs and a female communist spy. A very beautiful communist spy. "Now, if I can use your phone, Captain, I need to report in."

"Absolutely." He turned the phone on his desk to face me and went off to find a private to start the typing. I'd just made a hell of a lot of paperwork for some joe, but too bad for him.

I reached for the phone slowly and held it in a clenched fist while I contemplated what I was going to say. Nothing came to mind. I'd just have to wing it like I'd done most everything else. One ring, two rings…three.

The voice was familiar. "Hello…hello, who is this?"

"Mr. Reynardie, Sir, it's me, Shawn Riggs."

There was a pause as he sucked in some air and let it out slowly. "Where are you, son?"

"Berlin, Sir. I'm in Berlin."

"Okay, Shawn. Let me have it. What's going on?"

I didn't answer him. I wanted to, but I couldn't. Instead…instead, I just cried. Tears flew out of my eyes, and I bawled like a little baby. I tried to speak, but words wouldn't come. Finally, when my throat went dry, and my eyes could no longer see, I simply said, "I fucked up, Sir. I'm sorry."

His voice held no malice. "It's okay, Shawn. We can fix this. You're not the only guy who's ever made a mistake. Now, where in Berlin are you?"

"I'm at an army post, D Company, 2nd of the 6th Infantry, in the S2's office. I'm making my report."

"Good." He paused. "I'm betting this isn't something you can talk to me about over an open line?"

"Oh, no."

He chuckled, "Figures. You just hang tight, son. We got you now. Let me talk to that S2."

I handed the phone to Captain Fredrick. The two officers chatted amicably, but I just tuned out. I was beyond exhausted. When the phone call ended, the captain offered me his office couch, and I didn't argue. Collapsing on the old leather cushions, I passed out.

***

The dream seemed so real. Riding a blood-red horse, I crossed the prairie and continued up the canyon wall, my cowboy hat now gray; I remember that clearly. But nothing else made sense. My six gun was empty, so I threw it away and watched it skip off a canyon rock. Then, I looked in my holster and saw the six-gun was still on my hip. I threw it away. It skipped on a rock. I looked and saw it on my hip. I threw it away....

***

"Wake up, Sergeant. Sergeant, wake up!"

My eyes slowly opened to see an MP standing over the couch with a billy club in his hand. His face rang a bell. "Hello, Private Ackles."

"Hello, Sergeant Riggs." Smiling a wicked grin, he added, "You need to come with me now."

Well, this was inevitable. I got up slowly. My back and shoulders snapped and cracked like a bowl of Rice Krispy's. I took a moment to straighten my tie before offering him my wrists. He slapped handcuffs on 'em and took me outside for an early morning stroll. The friendly Captain Fredrick was nowhere to be seen.

The sun shown warm upon my face and the birds sang happily as I hobbled along in my one shoe towards imprisonment. A few GIs started, but most looked away, probably figuring I was none of their business; and besides, chow was being served at the dining hall. If that's what they thought, I had to say they were right—I was none of their fucking business.

Of course, the stockade looked very familiar to me.

When I walked in the joint, the whole room got quiet as a tomb while every MP stopped and stared. Corporal Witherspoon spilled his coffee as his cup nearly tumbled out of his hand. Ackles, smiling like the cat who'd caught the canary, emptied my pockets and put everything in a canvas bag. When he discovered I was wearing a shoulder holster, he asked, "Where's your weapon."

"Taking a swim," I answered.

"Okay, smart ass, come this way." Strutting past the desks, he led me beyond the coffee maker and through the rear door, where they did indeed keep the jail cells…two even rows of three cells each separated by a walkway. He put me in the middle one on the left. A door slam and a key turn later, I was confined in an eight by eight cage with a sink, a toilet, and an old battered army cot.

"How about these?" I asked as I held up my cuffed wrists.

Ackles just snickered and walked away.

Across from me sat a caged master sergeant. He wore a torn khaki uniform, and his bloodshot eyes and busted lip told the story of how he'd spent last night. He asked, "What're you in for?"

I let out a snort. "Stupidity."

He nodded. "Ain't we all, buddy? Ain't we all."

Making use of the small sink and the toilet, I was thankful the cell didn't have a mirror this time. Well, Mom and Dad, your son's a jailbird; just like Uncle Patrick. There was a clock on the wall by the entrance door. At eight that morning, they fed the master sergeant and I a good breakfast of eggs, sausage, and grits.

At ten twenty-three, they beat the ever-loving shit out of me.

Captain Padalecki opened the festivities when he swaggered in the room with his toady trailing behind. "Private Ackles, open this door. I need to have a talk with the prisoner."

"Yes, Sir!" The private was absolutely jubilant as he turned the key.

The barrel-chested officer strode in and asked me just one question. "Special Agent Riggs, do you know how much trouble you've caused me?"

He didn't wait for an answer. A right hook connected with my left cheek and the party began in earnest. I'm not sure how many times the gorilla slugged me, but I was pretty sure he enjoyed it; he was laughing the whole damn time.

My face got pounded pretty good. The swelling on my chin got split right open, and a couple of teeth on my right side gave up and left town before it was over. Finally, he paused for air. I collapsed to the floor and got a short break to drool on the cement.

"Well, Private, don't just stand there." He smiled while he talked. The bastard still smiled. "Help the prisoner to his feet."

The captain stepped aside to make way for the private's size seven boot to rocket into my gut. Out came the eggs, sausage, and grits in a puddle on the floor. I looked up to see the boot returning for another visit and squirmed over the remains of my breakfast to avoid it. He missed me, which only pissed him off more; a billy club cracked across my back and drove my collarbone into the concrete as my vision blurred.

Everything went black.

When I came to, my eyes were so swollen I could barely see the clock on the wall. Squinting, I made out twelve noon. Gingerly rolling into a sitting position, I smelled the stale vomit now covering my clothes and groaned.

In the next cell, crouching as far away as he could get, the master sergeant looked at the ceiling and shook his head. "I ain't seen nothin."

CHAPTER THIRTEEN

At twelve forty-five the medic showed up, a clean-cut kid in green fatigues with a white armband that bore the Red Cross. "Buddy, you look like hell."

I had to agree with him, but I was too weak to do more than nod.

"They told me you 'fell.' I'm here to take a look at you, okay?"

Again, I nodded as Corporal Witherspoon stepped up to unlock the door. Witherspoon carried a bucket with some soapy water and a sponge. The medic carried an aid bag. While Witherspoon removed my handcuffs, the good doc shined a light in my eyes. "Well, despite all the bumps on your head, you ain't got no concussion. That's good. Why don't you get out of those clothes and just kick 'em out of the cell? We got a fresh set of fatigues here for you, Sergeant."

Sergeant? The kid knew my rank at least. Witherspoon handed me a folded set of olive-drabs with a fresh change of underwear, socks, and boots. The uniform lacked any rank, and the boots were new issue stiff, but they weren't soaked in sweat and puke, so I wasn't complaining. The medic helped me up. With all the parts of me that hurt, it took forever to get out of the brown suit, washed up, and into the uniform.

"Now, Sarge," the medic said as he handed me the socks, "let's see about some of those cuts."

Iodine stings, and before it was over, my face and left foot felt like they just met a beehive. But, I had soft cotton pressed against my wounds and gauze wrapped around half my mug, so I called it an improvement.

"Thank you," I managed.

The kid chuckled. "You'll get my bill. I'm a practicing that line, you see? Gonna be a big shot doctor when I get out of this here army. Just you see."

I smiled, and it hurt. "Mack, you can patch me up any day."

The kid gave me a thumbs-up, packed his aid bag, and left. Witherspoon locked my cell as he told me, "Lunch is in about ten minutes, Sergeant."

I nodded as I rolled over on my cot. Lunch in ten minutes; and what would happen to Mrs. Riggs little boy after that?

***

"Hey, Sergeant, you're out of here. Command says they're not pressing any charges." It was Private Ackles carrying a cell key. The key went into the master sergeant's lock.

Slowly the old soldier rose from his cot. "And the waitress? She ain't pressing charges neither?"

"Beats me, Sarge. I was just told you were to report to your commander for company action. The Berlin Police never returned our calls. But, if I were you, I'd avoid that restaurant from now on."

The man nodded as he rubbed his sore lip. "I won't be going back. That girl packs a mean wallop."

As the master sergeant walked out of the cellblock, Ackles just turned and sneered at me. Gosh, some guys really carry a grudge! I closed my eyes and went back to pretending I was asleep while my tongue kept searching for my missing back teeth. Three hours later, I still hadn't found them. Truth be told, there's not a lot to do in a cell.

"Hey, Dickhead!" My eyes opened up to see the sneering private by the door. "Turns out there's someone to see you."

In walked a man in a light gray summer suit with a pink tie. He carried a briefcase in one hand and in his other held a badge raised for me to see. "Special Agent Myers, US Army Counterintelligence Corps. Are you Shawn Riggs?"

I sat up. "Yep, that's me."

The door shut as Ackles departed—good riddance. Myers pulled up a chair outside my cell and looked around. We were alone; the briefcase opened and out came a notebook and pencil. "I'm here to take your report."

"My what?"

"Your report. Technically, it's my report, I guess, but I plan to put your name on it. I'm not the kind of guy to take credit for another agent's work."

I liked this guy.

"Okay." My mind started on the outline. "What exactly does G2 want to know about?"

Myers looked at me as if I were stupid. Looking dumb, however, never bothered me. I actually just needed a moment to think. There would be some things I didn't want in any report.

"You're a counterintelligence man," he said. "Just give me the scoop. We got the stuff from the Brit, and the Russian transcripts have been translated. Now we need to know how you got that stuff, plus any other information you gained of intelligence value during Operation Paul Revere."

"Operation what?" I asked.

The man in the suit shrugged. "That's what it got called when your chief sent up the word that you were in pursuit of Nigel Leer, code named: Red Coat."

"Cute." Well, they had to call it something. "Okay, Myers, I'll take it from the top." I gave him everything…almost. To be frank, there were a lot of things I wasn't proud of; but this wasn't a confession, it was a report. All the army cared about was the information I could provide regarding our Communist foes. We weren't exactly enemies with the Russians, but we sure as hell weren't allies anymore, and America couldn't afford another Pearl Harbor.

Myers and I talked for over four hours. He asked a lot of good questions, and I tried to answer everyone…well, almost every one. I didn't tell about the killing of Uncle Joe and Curly Stooge—neither of 'em would affect national security anymore anyway. Of course, if I couldn't confess to killing two burly thugs, there was no way I was going to admit to killing Romana. Some things were just too secret to make their way into a report, no matter how classified.

So, I danced around the details. I think Myers suspected I had something to hide, but after a few attempts, he quit trying to get it out of me. He had plenty of typing to do as it was. After he had checked over his notes with me, he put the notebook back in the briefcase.

"Well, that's about it, Shawn. Thanks for all your help." He shook my hand through the bars. "And good luck, buddy."

I smiled as I gave his hand a firm squeeze. "Thanks, I need it."

***

"What happened to your face?" Reynardie asked.

"They tell me I fell."

He shook his head. I saw anger wash over him like a rogue wave, but he knew there was nothing he could do to change what was done. "You know, Shawn, I wish I'd never sent you to that damn train station."

It was the Fourth of July. Chief Reynardie had flown into Berlin with a USO troop on an old B-17 bomber to see his lost agent. He brought my mail and best regards from my teammates back in Paris.

I nodded. "I bet Ecklan's having a big laugh over this."

"Actually, he isn't. In fact, he hasn't said a bad word about you since you went missing. Your buddy Sands has been worried sick. Called his dad in the State Department I don't know how many times."

"Sands is a good friend," I admitted.

"I talked to First Sergeant McGuire. Actually, I talked to him a lot these past weeks. He kept you off the AWOL list as long as he could, but when Captain Shoemaker came back from leave, he didn't give McGuire a choice. You've officially been absent without leave for nine days."

"Thank you, Chief."

He nodded. "I do what I can. The thing I couldn't help you with was that charge of aiding and abetting an escape from the stockade." Shaking his head, he added, "Son, that one's gonna cost you."

Rolling my eyes, I gave him a nod and took a sip of my coffee. It was good stuff; French press from the Notre Dame market. Reynardie had brought it in his thermos all the way from Paris. Very nice of him.

"Still, you did a first class job busting Leer out." He smiled. "When I think of how rough some of our operations were back in Italy during the war, and here you go, all by your lonesome. They tell me you were cool as a cucumber, just sipping coffee with 'em while that captain of theirs got madder and madder."

I chuckled. I guess I did a pretty good job at that. But I'd made a few mistakes that day as well.

"Too bad you used General Clay's name on those orders you forged."

"Yep," I said. "I figured it worked when I requisitioned that office furniture back at Camp St. Germaine."

His eyes got big when he remembered my couch and tables. "Oh Christ, Shawn. Don't mention that. I think you're in enough trouble as it is."

We both had a good hard laugh about that. It'd been a long time since I'd laughed and it felt real good. When we settled down, Reynardie looked left and right over his shoulder. The master sergeant hadn't been replaced by any new inmates; we were still alone.

"Shawn, are you sure that Leer guy was on the level?"

I shrugged. "In this business it's impossible to be one-hundred percent sure about anybody," I answered. "But yes, Sir, I believe he's on our side."

"Well, that information he gave you was pretty hot. The reports he wrote not so much, but those phone conversations about blew the roof off G2. They confirm what we've suspected. The Soviet leadership is sticking to our wartime agreement and won't interfere with flights into Berlin. That's exactly what the brass hats needed to get the politicians to sign off on Operation Vittles."

"What?" And I thought Operation Paul Revere sounded dumb.

"Shawn, we're flying in everything needed to keep Berlin alive. Coal, wheat, children's toys, you name it. The Ruskies have flown some interference to pester us, but they haven't shot at a single Allied plane. Looks like the Reds are the suckers this time. We're keeping Berlin!"

Outside the MPs were having an Independence Day barbecue. I could smell the hot dogs. The smoke from the grill wafted through the window. At least somebody was enjoying the holiday.

"They're going to fly everything into Berlin?" I asked. "That's got to take a hell of a lot of doing."

"Hey, son, remember we're Americans. We can do anything!"

I smiled. A WOP from New York just told a mick from Boston that we could do anything. Maybe that was true? Maybe some hillbilly dogface from Alabama and a Negro truck driver from Indianapolis could accomplish miracles—just by being Americans together. Maybe we'd lick the Russians and liberate Stieglitz someday; maybe rescue the woman with the wooden smile too. Maybe.

Anything was possible. That was, with the exception of getting one screw-up spook out of the clink. Too bad for me.

We finished the coffee in silence. When Private Brewer came to lock up the cell, my old boss shook my hand and left. "Shawn, I read your report. You did a good job."

"Thank you, Sir." He was a good man to work for. But I knew I'd never see him again. Damn shame really; good bosses were hard to find.

My mail he left on the cot. The first letter was from my dad.

***
Dear Shawn,

We have not heard from you in a while. I know you must be busy, but your mother worries. On Sunday, Father Mike said a special prayer for our boys who are still overseas. I told him I appreciated him thinking of you. Just send us a postcard when you can, Shawn. Your mother worries.

I do have some good news. Bugs got me a job as a truck driver for Brinks! I start next week and have the uniforms and everything. I will be dressed like a cop, but who cares? A job is a job and this one I can feel good about. Bugs said I did not owe him anything, but I know how things work. He is running for city council this coming election and now he has got the whole Riggs clan voting for him. With all your cousins and uncles, he will be a shoe in. I will make sure you get that absentee ballot in time.

Jobs are still scarce over here, me boy. You hang in there for another year and maybe, by the time you get discharged, things will be looking up. And hey, how about those Sox! Looks like the pennant is ours this year.

Be careful over there. And, like I said, tell your buddy, Fred, to buy his own damn cigarettes from now on. Or did you do that already?

Love, Dad

***

Dad...I thought, as I clutched the letter in my hands, I love you too!

***

When you're charged with aiding and abetting an escape, the MPs don't like to take chances. They chained me from ankle to wrist, and it took four soldiers with grease guns to walk with me to the motor pool. They were joking and enjoying the fresh morning air, taking long strides, while I hopped with my feet chained only a foot apart. I had to do a kind of hop, step, hop, step routine to keep up with 'em, which the MPs thought was funny as hell.

The sun was warm, and the sky over Berlin clear—except for all the airplanes. I never saw anything like it. One after another swept down toward Tempelhof. The airlift was in full swing, and there'd be no more panicked Berliners hoarding groceries or black vans with speakers. Just a normal summer day in the city, compliments of Operation Vittles.

The MPs drove me to the old red brick building that used to have my old office; the same building complex that housed the headquarters of General Lucius Clay. I hoped like hell that I wasn't about to meet the son-or-a-bitch face to face. I had enough friends.

It was hard going up stairs with the leg shackles, but my MP escort didn't seem to have much pity. One said, "Come on, little bunny. Hop!" and the others gave a big laugh.

Fine, I thought, you assholes try this sometime. Three flights up and then a left. The hallway led to an office with the words Judge Advocate General painted on the door's glass windowpane.

Inside the room my eyes beheld a smallish office; just a couple of wooden chairs and a table, lit by a single lamp hanging from the ceiling. There were no other doors or windows. The MP shut the door behind me and waited outside.

I hate waiting. Nothing to read and nothing to do. I had a bad cigarette craving, but somehow guessed the GIs on the other side of the door would just laugh if I tried to bum a smoke. "Bum," there was a word. Of all the insults in the one language I knew, "bum" was probably the worst. A useless, washed up person; smelly and unwanted. Even though I was clean just then, in every other sense, I knew…I was a bum. And worse, a murderous bum; but I was the only one who knew that. Well, me and a guy named Nigel knew it, and Lord knew his whereabouts at that moment. Moscow maybe? Wherever, I hoped he got what he wanted. I hoped he was free.

I looked back at the door and read Judge Advocate General in backwards script on the frosted glass. Huh, I mused; in general, I knew judgment was coming, but where was my advocate? It seemed the army forgot to issue me one.

The door opened.

He was a clean-cut gentleman who looked to be in his mid to late fifties. His dark blue pinstripe suit was impeccable, and the yellow tie matched the pocket-handkerchief exactly. Under his left arm, he carried a thick manila folder. On the cover were the words: Sergeant Shawn Riggs, Special Agent, US Army, Secret//No Foreign.

The guy took a seat across the table from me and put on a pair of old-fashioned spectacles. He didn't look up, just opened the file to the first page. "My name is Hubert Sands. I believe you know my son."

My jaw dropped so low it almost smacked against the tabletop. "Pleased to meet you, Mr. Sands."

He glared over the spectacles at me. "Sergeant, you are one pain in my ass. I have no idea what my boy sees in you. I'm just glad you didn't contrive to embroil him in this mess. You, Sergeant, are an inconvenience."

"Sorry, sir. I didn't mean to be."

"Well, what did you mean to be?" he insisted. "Some kind of hot shot maybe?"

Shaking my head, I replied, "No, Mr. Sands I...was just trying to do a good job and...things got out of hand. It's my fault, sir. All of it. I know."

Mr. Sands shook his head. "Not quite all your fault, Sergeant. You didn't let a homosexual into the ranks of British intelligence back in 1943, did you?"

"No, sir."

"Then that one's not on you." His eyes went back to the folder. "Nevertheless, that homosexual seems to be a very talented field operator. I'm sure you have a good idea of just how effective he was."

Nodding, I answered, "Nigel was the best spy I'll ever know."

"Hmm," he nodded back.

"And he's loyal, sir," I added.

"Shame we couldn't keep him." He turned a page in the file. "But, you're right, it seems he's working for our side still. Working very hard indeed, and without a pension, I might add. I can't tell you much, just to say he's been in contact with some of our people in the East recently, and he's still sending us good information."

"Yes, sir. That's what he told me he was going to do. I think he felt it was a mistake that MI6 let him go, and he was out to prove that."

Mr. Sands turned another page in the folder. "Yes, and the information he provided has been confirmed by other sources. But the question right now is; what do we do about you?"

I didn't answer.

He looked up from the folder and gazed into my eyes. "Do you think it was a mistake that the army locked you up?"

Lowering my head, I answered, "No, sir. I'm getting what I deserve."

For the first time, Mr. Sands seemed to notice the bruises on my face. He grimaced like he smelled rotten meat or something. "How can you say that, Sergeant, when you don't even know what you are getting?"

What? "I'm getting court-martialed and sent to Fort Leavenworth, sir. I went AWOL and sprung a foreign spy from an army stockade."

"And lost your weapon," he added.

"Huh?" Then I remembered. "Oh, yes. I lost my weapon too."

He closed the folder. "Well, if General Clay had his way you'd probably be given the Silver Star, then shot by a firing squad on the same afternoon. He wasn't very happy when some lower enlisted soldier in the Counterintelligence Corps forged his name to commit a crime against the US Government. But, he was tickled pink when those phone transcripts confirmed that he was right about the airlift idea all along. Nothing a general likes more than being proven right, I suppose. So, like I said, first the metal then the execution would be his preference."

"And...what's really going to happen to me, sir?"

Reaching back into the file, he produced a document and placed it on the table before me. In bold letters on the top of the page, it read: Discharge Under Other Than Honorable Conditions from the Armed Forces of the United States of America.

"You're going home, Mr. Riggs. Anything harsher than the OTH discharge, like a Bad Conduct Discharge or whatnot, would require a court-martial. Court martials are messy, Mr. Riggs, and involve a lot of people. Mark my words, no one concerned wants to make any of this affair more public than we have to. Now, anything less, like an honorable discharge, would be an affront to military discipline; at least, that's what General Clay said about it. Believe me, Shawn. I did my best for you."

I couldn't blame him at all. It was better than I expected and certainly better than I deserved. I tried to give him my hand, but the chains wouldn't let it reach across the table. He circled around and shook it anyway.

I said, "Thank you, sir. And please tell Fred I said 'thanks' to him too."

The old diplomat smiled and gave me a wink that was almost Irish. "I will, Shawn," he said, and added, "He said he owed you for all the cigarettes. And the best of luck to you."

CHAPTER FOURTEEN

"Jesus, Mary, and Joseph, I can't believe it!"

"Watch your language, Arnie!" my mom called from the living room.

Dad threw the paper down on the kitchen table and looked me in the eye. "And they lost it in Fenway Park, the bums. Lost to the Cleveland goddamned Indians in Fenway Park! Whole season shot; it breaks my heart, boy, it truly does."

I picked up the Boston Globe, October 5th, 1948. Yep, Ted Williams notwithstanding, the curse of the Bambino was still in effect. The Berlin Airlift was in effect as well, although it had moved to page three. Blockading the city just wasn't working out for the Ruskies. Well, at least general Clay was happy. Stalin sure as hell wasn't. Too bad for him. But too bad for Boston; there'd be no World Series for the Sox this year.

I put the paper down and went back to playing with my eggs. Dad had gotten up early after working the night shift to make me breakfast. He burnt the toast, and the coffee tasted like dishwater—it felt good to be home.

"Well, Shawn, it's just as well you didn't want to go to the game. Game like that. I tell you."

"Yeah, Dad," I said.

"You know, Shawn, you can tell your pops when you're ready. Right? I mean, I won't hold nothing against you." He'd said this about three times a day, every day, since I arrived home from Fort Dix two weeks ago. That's where the army sent me for assignment to the Returnee Reassignment Section for my out processing. I was confined to a barracks with a bunch of thugs and losers for five weeks while the paperwork ground through the army's mill. Then they'd sent me home on a Greyhound bus wearing a baby blue suit.

"You know," Dad went on, "I talked to Father Mike. If you don't want to tell me, that's okay too. But at least give your problems to God, boy."

That almost got a smile out of me. "I tried that once, Dad."

"You did?" Now the old man seemed excited. "That's good. That's very good. What did the priest have to say?"

I shrugged. "Something in Czechoslovakian."

He frowned. "I thought you were in France or Germany the whole time. How was it you were in Czechoslovakia?"

The eggs were runny, but I took a big bite anyway. I didn't answer his question. The army made it clear; I was to divulge nothing of my trip east, ever. Mentioning Czechoslovakia was a slip-up. I'd try not to repeat it, but I wasn't about to start lying to my dad either. So I just kept quiet. I'd been doing that a lot lately, and it was really driving him nuts. I hadn't figured out how to help him with that problem just yet, though.

I hadn't figured out a lot of things, for that matter.

Dad got up and opened the kitchen window for some air. It was a clear day, and we could plainly see the top half of the Bunker Hill Monument. I used to play around that thing all the time as a kid. We'd pretend we were Irish Republicans fighting the British as they advanced up the hill. Some kid would invariably get to play the general and shout, "Don't fire until you see the whites of their eyes!"

Or the back of her coat.

I picked up the paper and turned to the want ads. Things were picking up some, and there were a few jobs that suited me; taxi driver, dishwasher, fry cook, night watchman. Every day I'd look at the ads and circle a half dozen. Then I'd call a few. Trouble was nobody wanted to hire a guy who got chucked out of the army on his ass. There were a lot of veterans applying for jobs back then, and most of them had clean discharges.

Dad got a beer out of the fridge and pulled the top. The pop and fizz wasn't very loud, but from the living room we heard, "Arnie, are you drinking beer before noon again?"

"No, love," he shouted back. "Just getting one for Shawn." With a thump, a fresh beer appeared on the table by my coffee.

Oh, hell, I might as well. As I took a pull on the long-necked bottle of Point Special, the phone rang.

"Shawn!" my mother called. "It's for you."

Stepping into the living room, I saw my mom on the overstuffed couch with the phone in her hand. When she saw the beer bottle in mine, she frowned but said nothing...she didn't have to. I put the beer down on the coffee table and picked up the phone.

"Hello, this is Shawn."

"Mr. Riggs, my name is Cumberland. I'm in Boston this week doing some recruiting, and I was wondering if I could talk to you."

I blinked. "This is about a job?"

"Yes, sir, it is."

"I don't want to waste your time, Mr. Cumberland. I have a bad discharge from the army."

"Oh, sir, that's not a problem." The guy practically smiled through the receiver. "Tell me; since you got out of the service, have you found a job you like?"

"No."

"Well, I understand times are hard. Can I visit you at your home? Say tomorrow at three o'clock?"

What was this guy's angle? "Sure."

"Very well. Am I correct that you live at 150 Lincoln Street, Apartment C?"

"Yes." How did he know who I was and where I lived? I connected the dots...they weren't very far apart; army discharge records...this guy was probably government. Was he deliberately looking for guys who got kicked out? That would be unusual, to say the least.

"Swell, I will see you tomorrow." The line went click.

My mother was busy watering the plants in the garden box with Point Special beer. "Are you having friends over?"

"Mom," I said, "I honestly have no idea."

***

The apartment was spotless. All that day Mom spent cleaning and dusting. "We have to make a good impression, Shawn. You can't mope about the house forever. You need to find yourself a job."

"Mom," I said. "I don't even know who this guy is or what kind of job he's offering."

"Doesn't matter, Shawn. A job's a job."

My dad was a bit more skeptical and spent the day on the phone asking questions of people in the know. "Shawn, do you know this Cumberland guy from the army or something?"

"No, Dad."

"I didn't think so. I didn't think so. You know, I talked to Bugs. He's never heard of this guy either. But the guy's not connected, and he isn't working for the city either."

I let out a sigh. "Dad, I told you, he said he was in Boston for only a week, so he's an out-of-towner."

"Okay, okay, but if he's a Fed, Bugs would know that too." Dad snorted. "I bet every fucking G-man in the city's on the take."

From the bedroom, we heard Mom yell. "Watch your language, Arnie!"

"I said, 'trucking,' love! Can't you see I'm going to work?" Actually, my dad didn't have to be at work until five, and that meant he usually left to take the MTA at four o'clock. But he was already wearing his Brinks uniform, with the .38 caliber revolver at his side. His shoes were shined to a warm, soft glow.

I wore tan chinos and a white shirt. I had a suit coat that matched but had left it in the closet. Mom, however, insisted I wear a tie. She came into the living room with a plaid red and green number. "I got this for your father while you were away, but he never wears it. It's got the Riggs family tartan."

I took the tie. "Mom, we're Irish. I thought wearing a family plaid was a Scottish thing."

She shrugged. "It was St. Patrick's Day, and the man at the store was so nice. Wear the tie, Shawn. It'll bring you luck for your job interview."

She kissed me on the cheek.

"Okay, Mom."

I liked the tie. It was a little bright, but the hell with it. This was my house! I'd wear whatever I wanted. After all, I wasn't in the army anymore.

I checked my watch...fourteen forty-eight. No, Goddamn it...it was twelve to three! From now on civilian time only for Shawn Riggs. With twelve minutes to kill, I went to the kitchen to make a pot of coffee. After all, when this guy Cumberland arrived, I might as well be polite and offer him a cup.

Just when I got the pot brewed, a knock was heard at the door—and I spilled coffee on my tie. Shit. Well, it could have been worse...my white shirt was spared. Hoping nobody would notice the wet spot on the tartan, I stepped out of the kitchen with a fresh pot of joe in one hand and a couple of mugs in the other.

Mom was opening the door while Dad took up a position between the couch and the easy chair. My mother was all smiles as she said, "Welcome, Mr. Cumberland and...."

Cumberland took off his fedora and introduced his colleague. "This is Mr. Hatch, ma'am. A pleasure to make your acquaintance."

The two men stepped into the living room in their bland suits. They were each in their mid-thirties with perfect hair and had the look of Harvard college boys all grown up.

"And I'm glad to meet you," Mom replied. "This is...." She turned to Dad to see him glaring at her guests. Her tone hardened as she stared at him, "My husband, Mr. Riggs. Unfortunately, he has to leave for work now."

Dad didn't say a word, and he didn't have to. He just stared at them with a look that had terrified punks on the South Side for decades. Its meaning was clear; don't mess with my boy.

When the two men's faces broadcasted, "message received." Dad put on his peaked cap and went out the door without saying a word.

"And this is my son, Shawn." Mom indicated me.

The two men nodded as I set the coffee on the table. I nodded back and said, "Hi," like only the Americans do. "Want some coffee?"

Cumberland said, "No thank you." But Hatch took a cup, black, no sugar. I poured myself one, dropped in a spoonful of sugar, then took a seat on the couch.

Cumberland turned to my mother. "Mrs. Riggs, I'm sorry, but we need to speak to your son in private. Is that possible?"

My mom took a moment to think it over. "Why, yes. I'll just go on up to Mrs. Barragan's apartment. She and I need to discuss some things regarding the church calendar anyway."

Mom went to the bookshelf, grabbed her church notebook, smiled to one and all, and then left to visit our neighbor. A pregnant pause later, Cumberland handed me his card. It announced that he was John A. Cumberland, Intelligence Officer, Central Intelligence Agency, Tempo A, Washington, DC.

"Yeah," I said. "I thought you two might be spooks. Your suits are nice, but not too nice. I bet you blend in with just over half the guys walking around Boston today."

They both shifted in their seats a little. "So you've heard of us?"

"Nope," I answered truthfully. "But you've heard of me. I figured this had something to do with the government. The army already punished me, all right? And I never broke any law in the United States, so what's this about?"

"Actually," Hatch chimed in, "the United States is the one place our agency doesn't have any jurisdiction. You're not in trouble, Mr. Riggs. Not with us."

Cumberland nodded. "We're not the police, and we're not the military. The CIA is the nation's principal intelligence agency."

"Then how come I never heard of you?" I asked.

Cumberland pressed on. "Because we're new. Very new, Mr. Riggs. We only came into being by Act of Congress last year, along with the air force and a few other things. Our job is to pool all the resources of the other US intelligence agencies, like the army, FBI, the navy, and everybody else. We give the whole American intelligence community a place to send their reports, so they can all be analyzed together in a cohesive whole."

My eyebrows reached across my forehead to shake each other's hand. "So, you don't do any field work? You just sit in Washington at this," I held up the card, "Tempo A, and compare notes with all the other services."

"Well...." Cumberland squirmed.

Hatch pushed in. "That's what we're supposed to do. For now, just analysis work. But some of us have bigger ideas."

"Yes, that's right," Cumberland added. "We don't have any field operators yet, but we see that in the future we might need some. So we're trying to recruit people with experience. People who fought in the war, principally with the various resistance groups, or who worked in the OSS—"

"...or served in the Counterintelligence Corps," I finished for him.

"Precisely," he finished.

"You guys know who I am. You have access to my service record. Are you sure you want a failure pitching for your team?"

"Humph," Hatch grunted. "If you're a failure, I'm Mary Queen of Scotts. Riggs, you went deep into Communist-held territory, remained undetected despite the language barrier, ran an operation without support, and brought back some of the most valuable intelligence of this past year. And you did it with minimal training and no cover identity, not even a false passport."

"I had help," I interjected.

Hatch was undeterred. "The Limey? How did you know you could even trust him? Not bringing him in was the right call, but how many guys would see it that way? And then the self-executed operation you did to spring him from a military lock up—very impressive indeed."

"I broke some rules," I added.

Cumberland leaned back in my mom's chair. "We aren't the Boy Scouts of America, Mr. Riggs. The world is growing colder. The Russians are running the game on us from Asia to the Atlantic, and it's time we put our team in the field. This is a new kind of war, you see?

And it's the kind of war you've already fought in! We need men like you, who can break a few rules to get results. Otherwise, we just give the whole game to the Commies, and that's not an option. Not in this day and age. From your file, we learned a lot about the kind of man you are—and aren't."

Hatch said, "We can read between the lines, Riggs. You've done things that didn't make it into your report. What happened to your gun?"

That snapped me out of it. "My what?"

Hatch smiled. "Your .45 automatic, Riggs. The first time they put a weapon in your hand in basic training, I bet you were taught that a soldier is never without his weapon. Where's your gun?"

None of his goddamn business, that's where it was. "I lost it."

"Lost it? Or disposed of the evidence?" Hatch went on, "You were an expert marksman in basic training. Did you ever have a chance to test those skills in the real world?"

"No."

Hatch smiled. "You're a good liar, too. See, we could use a man like you."

"It's a good paying job, Mr. Riggs," Cumberland said. "We can even fix your problem with the army. Make that less-than-honorable into an honorable discharge, promote you to staff sergeant, whatever. Your country needs men of your peculiar talents." He smiled a sideways grin; these guys could make things happen and knew it. "There should be no shame in that."

I thought about it from all angles. I really did. My decision, however, came quickly. I had the chance to go back, to be an agent again. I could travel the world, make good money, and lie to everyone I met in dozens of foreign cities. I might even meet a girl again. A very beautiful and exotic girl, with a tragic past.

I looked the government men in the eye. Each was as earnest as the day is long. Each had come all the way to Boston to find someone with rare experience; a soldier for their new clandestine war.

Giving it to them straight…I figured that was best. With guys like this you have to be absolutely clear.

I told them, "Go to hell."

THE END

ABOUT THE AUTHOR

Throughout his life, Clayton J. Callahan has made his living in the armed professions. In the 1980s he served in the US Navy with an anti-terrorist unit. After 9/11, he enlisted in the US Army and is now an Iraq War veteran twice over. Between deployments, he's worked as a deputy sheriff, a correctional officer, and as a federal agent for US Army Counterintelligence.

Callahan's writing tends to stress the human element of every story he tells. He believes that people want to connect with people through fiction. Therefore, he strives to make his characters as interesting and as human as possible. He does this through his own unique sense of humor and life experiences. As most of his life experiences revolve around soldiers, police officers, spies, and criminals, such people feature prominently in his work. In this, he puts stereotypes aside, making each and every character someone real enough to have a story all unto themselves.

He is primarily considered a science fiction writer. However, Callahan has also written historical spy fiction, ghost stories, and non-fiction books.

Other Books by Clayton J. Callahan

Made in United States
Troutdale, OR
11/05/2024

24461893R00110